POINT OF IMPACT

NUCLEAR DAWN BOOK ONE

KYLA STONE

PAPER MOON PRESS

Point of Impact

Copyright © 2018 by Kyla Stone All rights reserved. This book or any portion thereof may not be reproduced or used in any manner whatsoever without the express written permission of the publisher except for the use of brief quotations in a book review.

This book is a work of fiction. Any references to historical events, real people, or real places are used fictitiously. Other names, characters, places, and events are products of the author's imagination, and any resemblances to actual events or places or persons, living or dead, is entirely coincidental.

Printed in the United States of America

Cover design by Christian Bentulan

Book formatting by Vellum

ISBN: 978-1-945410-28-4

First Printed in 2018

 Created with Vellum

To Jeremy, for holding down the fort while I made up imaginary people in imaginary worlds.

1

DAKOTA

ZERO HOUR MINUS TWENTY MINUTES…

Dakota Sloane was no stranger to hardship. A born survivor, she'd spent her life waiting for the next calamity, the next disappointment, the next strike from a world intent on breaking her.

But Dakota didn't break.

She felt close now, though. Her chest tightened as she scanned the street outside the window of the Beer Shack Bar.

A damp rag in one hand, she froze, bent over a yellow table strewn with crumpled napkins and a greasy, half-eaten lunch of twist fries, burgers, and globs of ketchup.

Her gaze locked on a familiar figure striding through the lunchtime crowd strolling along Front Street in Overtown along the outskirts of downtown Miami.

She knew that confident, purposeful walk, the lean, lanky shape of him, sharp as a knife blade. She'd recognize that thin, angular face anywhere, those grim, fevered eyes—the eyes that haunted her nightmares.

He wasn't supposed to be there.

Dakota didn't believe in coincidences.

If Maddox Cage was in Miami—in this part of Miami—it was for one reason.

He was here for her. For her and Eden.

She'd made it two years and thirteen days. She wasn't ready yet, hadn't saved enough. Six more months and her plan would be in place, ready for execution.

Five grand and her little sister. That was all she needed to start a brand-new life a thousand miles away.

Miami was loud and colorful and always moving, made up of a jumble of Cubans, Haitians, Asians, South Americans, and Anglos, an exuberant smorgasbord of cultures, music, food, and art.

Miami was an easy city to get lost in.

But she hadn't gotten lost enough.

Sweat prickled along her hairline. She took a step back from the window, hoping the sunlight's glare on the glass would shield her presence.

Maybe he only had a general idea of their location. If he was still searching, if he didn't already know exactly where she was...

But maybe he wasn't coming for her first. The thought sent a cold fission of dread through her gut.

He was going after Eden.

She held her breath until he passed—never turning his head to the left or right, eyes fixed straight ahead as he weaved between the pedestrians thronging the sidewalk.

He always had been single-minded, like a dog with a bone.

She should've known he wouldn't let go. Would never let go.

She leaned over the table to get a better view of the street. Maddox Cage paused at the corner and waved down a taxi. Dakota didn't move until he slipped inside, shut the door, and the car pulled away from the curb.

"Excuse me, Miss," said a heavy, middle-aged Indian guy at the next booth.

She didn't know him. The usual regulars haunted their favorite bar stools, but this close to downtown and Miami International, the bar always served a steady stream of tourists and traveling business types.

People liked the Beer Shack's funky vibe. The bar was lined with kitschy shiny yellow tables and elephant palms in huge ceramic planters adorned with fairy lights.

Famous locations throughout Miami—South Beach, Freedom Tower, the Coral Castle Museum—were immortalized in bottle cap art hung on the faux brick walls.

The radio was always playing a vibrant mix of rumba, salsa, timba. The mix of authentic Cuban fare and classic American selections was damn good, too.

With his sweating mug of Sam Adams, the man gestured toward the flat-screen against the far wall. He was in his fifties and nearly bald, a neatly combed circle of white hair ringing his shiny brown scalp. "Can you turn that up?"

"Sure thing." She forced herself to move, to go through the motions, even as her mind spun with jostling, frantic thoughts.

She put the Coke glass down on the dirty table she'd been cleaning, leaving the plastic tub and rag behind. She pulled the remote from her moss-green apron and punched up the volume.

The Marlins' loss recap had been interrupted. The screen showed an aerial shot of Michigan Avenue in Chicago, completely cleared but for a minivan parked on the street.

Several police cars and SWAT vehicles were stationed a safe distance away, three helicopters hovering overhead.

A breathless, wide-eyed news reporter gesticulated wildly about something. She couldn't make sense of the woman's jumble of words.

"I live near the west side of Chi-Town. Heading back tomorrow. Crazy, huh?" the guy said.

"What's all the excitement about?" Dakota asked distractedly, forcing herself to be polite.

A low, frantic buzz filled her head.

Fear was already forming like ice around her heart.

She couldn't just leave in the middle of her shift. She couldn't afford to lose another job, but she had to contact Eden, had to figure out what to do.

"Some kind of bomb. Terrorist wackos, looks like. Probably ISIS. But Chicago PD caught it in time. Disarming it now, thank God."

"Good thing," she said.

He held his mug toward her. "Fill 'er up, would you?"

She grabbed the mug, refilled it at the bar, and returned it to the customer. He didn't acknowledge her. His eyes were glued to the screen.

Her nerves were stretched taut. Anxiety squeezed her lungs. She needed a break. She needed to reach Eden.

She strode across the room and paused, keeping her back to the empty bar-height table behind her, the glass front door on her left, the bar counter several feet to her right.

The bar wasn't busy yet. A handful of regulars hunched over their drinks, staring glassily at the second screen hung over the bar, showing the same view of the van in Chicago.

The steady buzz of their conversations was a constant hum in the background: Walter Monroe whining about his ex-wife; Jesse Peretti's grass kept dying from the increased water restrictions due to the drought; Tamara Santos complaining about more forced overtime.

Mendo Del Rio always brought up politics, especially when he was itching for a fight. The Beer Shack owner and current bartender, Julio de la Peña, had been forced to kick him out several times.

Most of the time, the regulars discussed sports and deep-sea fishing plans, crappy boss problems, and the latest indomitable heat wave.

They were all regular people with regular problems. No one was hunting them.

None of them paid any attention to her.

She jerked her cell out of her cargo pocket—an old model Samsung that barely qualified as a smartphone. It was all she could afford, since she put every extra penny toward her bug out fund.

As she tapped the contacts icon, she kept one anxious eye on the street outside, in case Maddox decided to double back. He was cunning like that.

Wanda Simpson, her sister's social worker, picked up on the fourth ring.

Dakota didn't waste time on greetings. "I need to see my sister. Now. Today."

"Well," the woman huffed. "I don't have time for this nonsense today, Ms. Sloane. You know as well as I do that you have court-appointed, *supervised* visits once a month and no more. Your next visit isn't for a week—"

"I can't wait that long."

"Ms. Sloane, your sister is medically fragile. She needs consistency. The judge, the psychologists, and I all agree that disrupting her carefully maintained routine would be detrimental to her well-being."

"Which is just shrink-speak for trying to keep me from my sister so you can adopt her out—"

Mrs. Simpson sighed heavily into the phone.

Dakota could hear voices in the background. At the bar,

someone turned the TV up even louder. She gritted her teeth, repressing everything she longed to say, pressed the cell to her ear, and turned away from the bar. "Look. It's an emergency."

The woman gave another imperious sigh, like she was already patting herself on the back for her boundless, saintly patience. "What kind of emergency, Ms. Sloane?"

Dakota couldn't tell the social worker who she'd seen or what she feared it meant. She'd never explained what she and her sister had escaped from. To bring Maddox up now would expose them both to questions they wouldn't—couldn't—answer.

"I just need to see her, okay?"

"I'm afraid I can't do that."

Frustration bubbled up inside her. She was already doing her best to do everything absolutely right.

First: gain steady employment and stable housing. Second: petition the courts for custody before Eden's rich, shiny foster parents sank their claws into her permanently and whisked her away with promises of a real family, vacations to the Keys, art and tennis lessons.

Until then, she kept to herself and stayed wary and watchful.

She saved every penny, spending nothing extra on herself other than her sessions three times a week at the gun range off Miami Avenue.

She carefully maintained a low profile—never attracting attention, avoiding conflict, even when she wanted to punch someone in the kidneys.

It was essential to remain under the radar at all times.

In two years, she'd begun to think that they'd escaped the horrors they'd fled, that the past wouldn't follow them.

But she was dead wrong.

The fragile sense of security she'd built around herself had shattered the moment her gaze snagged on Maddox Cage among the sweating crowds outside the bar windows.

"I'm practically her guardian!" she forced out. "I'll be ready to petition the court in a few months—"

"It would be foolish to make such an assumption, Ms. Sloane." Mrs. Simpson sniffed derisively. "It's not an appropriate—or healthy—frame of mind, especially considering your inability to maintain steady employment, your lack of a G.E.D. or high school diploma, and your...flexible...housing arrangements."

Dakota could imagine her smug face, her cheap polyester suits, that awful chemical perfume that smelled like burnt rubber. The woman despised Dakota and her "negative influence" over her fifteen-year-old sister.

A helpless fury roiled in her gut. "I've done everything you've asked. Gotten a job—"

"Bussing tables hardly qualifies as a job—"

"I have an apartment!"

"In a highly dangerous and questionable neighborhood."

She and Eden had been separated for almost two years, after they'd been caught sleeping on the sidewalks on Southeast First Street in downtown Miami.

With no parents and no family, the Florida Department of Children and Families—a terrible misnomer of a name if she'd ever heard one—had swallowed them up into its bloated, utterly broken foster care system.

After a slew of disastrous foster placements, Dakota was stuck in a group home for unwanted teens until she'd come of age eighteen months ago.

Her younger sister—beautiful, sweet, traumatized Eden—was placed in a specialized foster home for the medically fragile.

She swallowed back a curse. She couldn't afford to piss off a woman who still held so much power over her life.

"Please," she said instead, hating herself for begging, but giving it one last shot. If the woman still refused to help, she'd have to take matters into her own hands.

"You know I can't do that even if I wanted to, dear," Mrs. Simpson simpered. "And you know I only have your sister's best interests at heart…"

Behind Dakota, someone at the bar gasped. Dakota glanced back at the flat-screen. Her arm fell limply to her side. Her fingers barely held onto the phone.

The social worker babbled something, but Dakota wasn't listening anymore.

She could do nothing but watch the screen in stunned disbelief.

2

DAKOTA

ZERO HOUR MINUS FOUR MINUTES...

Cold went through Dakota all the way to her bones. The screen was split now—one side displaying the bomb squad descending on the minivan in Chicago; the other side, a shaky cellphone video of a massive cloud rising into the sky over a city so hazy with smoke, she couldn't tell which it was.

"...We repeat, we've just received reports from outside Washington, D.C. that there has been a massive explosion," the male reporter said, his voice rising in agitation.

The female reporter tapped her earpiece. "Communication is down in the area, but we've received information that a fireball at least a half mile wide has been sighted over Capitol Hill. It appears this is—this is an attack, Gerard. An attack on American soil..."

The first reporter's face drained of color. "It appears to be a bomb. A nuclear bomb."

The shot cut to the reporter on the street in Chicago. "We also have an unconfirmed report that the Michigan Avenue bomb is likely an improvised nuclear device, Gerard."

The newsdesk reporters didn't speak for a moment, the shock

and horror on their faces genuine. So often, the media seemed to feed on manufactured outrage or barely disguised gleeful delight in the "next big thing."

This, though, was beyond imaginable.

Dakota's own pulse thudded in her throat. Her chest tightened like some invisible hand was squeezing her heart.

"Ah," Gerard stammered, "so I'm hearing that we have multiple bombs. Multiple nuclear bombs—at least two. One has detonated in D.C. already. We've heard nothing definitive yet from official sources.

"Social media is blowing up with reports of a terrible explosion, though all locations are at least a few miles from the blast. We've had zero communication from anyone at the White House or Capitol Hill...Massive casualties must be expected..."

The patrons in the bar—five at the bar itself, three more in the booths—sat staring at the screens, frozen, their mouths agape.

Dread coiled in Dakota's gut. Slowly, she raised the phone to her ear. "Mrs. Simpson, are you watching the news? Check your phone."

"Really, Ms. Sloane," Mrs. Simpson huffed, "I don't have time for your games today. Some of us have actual work to do—"

"Another bomb!" the female reporter gasped. "We've just lost contact with large portions of New York. Hundreds—thousands of reports coming in on Twitter and social media. People reporting a massive mushroom cloud seen from miles away, buildings collapsing, massive fires..." Her voice trailed off in disbelief.

The second reporter gestured at someone offscreen before turning back to the cameras, visibly shaken. "We have a video feed. Please brace yourselves. This is live—"

The aerial shot revealed an enormous pillar of smoke larger than Dakota had ever seen, dwarfing the skyscrapers. She could barely see the skyline through all the smoke and fire.

Dakota took a step back, and then another, until her butt pressed against the lip of the bar table.

Three bombs. Not just bombs. Nukes.

Three targeted cities. New York. Washington D.C. Chicago.

Were there only three? Or were there more?

She thought of Ezra. He'd warned her of something like this.

What was it he always said? That smart terrorists would engage in a coordinated and multi-pronged attack. They would simultaneously attack the infrastructure—the electric grid, import hubs, or several cities—all intended to eviscerate American morale.

Just like this.

Dakota was a pessimist by nature. Experience had taught her that. Life always kicked you when you were already down.

Worst case scenario, more bombs were just waiting to be detonated. Miami wasn't the largest city in the U.S., but the metropolitan area was home to more than five million people. Seventh largest, her boss had said just last week.

Miami International Airport and the Port of Miami were also major hubs of commerce.

If there were more bombs, Miami was just as likely a target as any other.

An image bubbled up from somewhere deep inside her—a glimpse of a memory she'd shoved down deep. Something darkly, horribly familiar about all of this...

That feeling was in her, a cold dread creeping up her spine, tightening her chest, clawing at her throat. The hairs on her arms stood on end.

She'd learned to recognize it for what it was: a warning.

Dakota had to get out of the city. Right now.

"Mrs. Simpson, are you there? We're under attack. D.C. and New York just blew up."

"See? This is exactly what I mean. With your constant lying and toxic sarcasm, you're no proper role model for a child—"

"Where is Eden?"

"You know I can't tell you that."

Dakota struggled to remain calm, but all she wanted to do was reach through the phone and strangle the woman. "Where is she *now*? Call her foster parents. Tell them to get out of the city. Right now. Miami could be next!"

"That is simply ridiculous. Even if something's happened, it'd be irresponsible to incite a panic. The media does enough of that. I'm sure they're exaggerating as usual—"

"Just get her out, you good-for-nothing—" Dakota swallowed the curse and simply hung up on the social worker instead.

She'd get no help from the Florida Department of Children and Families. She was just wasting time.

She'd get Eden herself.

Luckily, she knew the foster parents' address, even though Mrs. Simpson had tried to keep it from her.

However, it was July seventh: smack-dab in the middle of a sweltering, unbearable Florida summer. Eden might be at her foster parents' home, at tutoring, or one of a half-dozen extracurriculars the fosters had signed her up for.

With shaking fingers, she punched in the number for the burner phone she'd smuggled to her sister last year.

She could only pray Eden had it with her.

No answer. She couldn't warn her about Maddox. That wouldn't work. She sent a quick text: *Ezra right. Bombs. Find shelter. I'm coming for you.*

When she looked up, most of the patrons were still sitting slack-jawed and stunned.

Only one had risen to his feet.

He was looking straight at her, frowning.

Logan Garcia was his name. Colombian, in his mid-twenties, he was a regular; always chatty with Julio, the bartender, but he'd never said much to her.

Logan was tall, lean, and muscular. He usually dressed in a loose black T-shirt and worn jeans. He had a tough, weathered look to him. His scruffy goatee lined a hard jaw beneath unkempt hair black as oil. Tattoos spiraled up both arms.

He always sat in the stool on the far left against the wall so he could watch the room. She'd seen him walk in, pause, scan the bar, and leave if that stool was already taken.

He had a sharp alertness about him—even with three or four drinks in him, even half-drunk—like he could snap to attention at the drop of a hat. The kind of guy who missed nothing.

He was also packing heat. She'd recognized the small bulge in the center of his back beneath his shirt. Logan Garcia wasn't exactly threatening, but he was powerful. Of that, she was certain.

He stared intently at her for a moment. It was unnerving, like he was seeing straight through her, sizing her up, taking in her anxiety, her apprehension.

She recognized a glint of something. A familiar wariness in his eyes, an awareness.

He was thinking the same thing she was: best to get the hell out of Dodge.

She nodded at him as she untied her apron. Julio wouldn't like it, but she was leaving. At least she had her bug out bag in her locker back in the staff room—the black, nondescript backpack she took everywhere with her, including work.

The bag carried her Springfield XD9, holster, spare 9mm ammo, and a grand in tens and twenties.

It also contained a Lifestraw water filter, water bottle, roll of duct tape, space blanket, solar electronic charger, fire starter, radio/flashlight combo, a compass and paper map of Florida, a few dozen meal replacement bars, and a medical kit.

The tactical knife, she kept on her person at all times.

She'd grab the bug out bag from the staff room and head the two and a half miles north to get her sister—social workers and foster parents be damned.

And then they'd do what they always did.

Run.

The double threat of Maddox Cage and now the bombs was too much. They weren't safe.

It wasn't how things were supposed to be. It wasn't the plan. But they'd survived by running twice before. They could do it again.

Her phone buzzed in her hand. It was from Eden. Three words: *Okay. At home.*

She was halfway down the aisle between the booths, heading for the staff room in the back to dump her apron and collect her things, when she felt it.

An icy breath on the back of her neck. A cold slither up her spine.

And then the world exploded.

3

LOGAN

ZERO HOUR MINUS TEN MINUTES...

Logan Garcia's main goal in life was to forget. The more you forgot, the better off you were.

Nothing helped him forget better than a stiff, cold drink.

The Beer Shack on Front Street was his go-to dive, though he visited numerous bars on a regular basis, sometimes more than a few in a single night. His pantry was stocked with Jack Daniels, Smirnoff, Bacardi, Johnny Walker—all his favorite friends.

He'd had a particularly vicious nightmare the night before.

Obviously, he hadn't gotten drunk enough. Usually, he was content to keep himself in a constant state of mild stupefaction.

He'd called in sick to his job at Thompson's Supply Chain Enterprises, where he worked as a forklift operator, loading and unloading delivery trucks from the main distribution center warehouse to various big box stores throughout Miami.

It was banal, mind-numbing work. But considering his circumstances, it was the best he could find. Not many companies wanted to hire him once they'd run the background check.

As soon as he'd dragged himself out of bed, still nursing a

hangover, he'd headed to his favorite bar, thirst burning the back of his throat, red bleeding behind his eyes.

He could always drink at home—and often did—but there was something about social drinking that served as that last tenuous thread connecting him to humanity.

He wasn't ready to sever it quite yet.

He swiveled toward the bar but kept his body angled, half-turned toward the door, facing the rest of the room to keep his sights on everyone. The usual regulars; a few suits killing time before another board meeting or flight. No threats.

He caught his reflection in the mirror behind the bar—his dark eyes were hooded, shadows bruising the hollows beneath them.

Without his usual mask of an easygoing smile, he looked like a man haunted.

He turned away, tilted his Corona, and drank half of it in one go.

He focused his attention on the highlights of the Marlins' game, chatting with bartender Julio de la Peña about his latest project: the 1968 Chevy Camaro he was restoring and repainting an electric lime green in his garage.

Beside him, Walter Burton—an ornery, grizzled regular with a ring of white hair fringing a pale, age-spot-speckled pate—started in on his litany of complaints against his ex-wife.

It was a typical Wednesday in July: the Miami humidity oppressive, the traffic awful.

Though it was earlier than he usually arrived, he easily slipped into the routine. A routine he'd come to appreciate, even enjoy.

At least, with what little joy he could still muster.

He hadn't paid attention to the news at first. It was all bad—what was the difference?

Not until seventy-year-old Walter halted mid-curse and raised his eyes to the screen. Not until Julio spilled white rum over the sides of the glass of the mojito he was making, liquid splattering all over his hands.

"What the living hell is this?" Walter growled in his raspy smoker's voice.

He lifted his Bud Light by the neck with a thumb and forefinger, tipped it back, and took several shaky gulps before smacking his lips and pointing the bottle at the flat-screen.

"Not since nine-eleven..." Julio stilled, just holding the mug, not even bothering to wash his hands.

His salt-and-pepper hair glinted beneath the bar lights, highlighting the tense lines around his mouth. In his early fifties, Julio's easy smile and open, earnest face kept him youthful, but he looked like he'd aged a decade in the last sixty seconds.

"I have a feeling this is going to be much, much worse." Logan felt sick, dread crawling up his throat, sucking at the corners of his mind. He knew that feeling well. He hated it.

It was the feeling he'd spent most of the last four years trying desperately to escape.

He swallowed down a gulp of Corona. He wasn't nearly drunk enough to survive this day.

"It's gotta be ISIS!" said a woman in her forties sitting at the end of the bar. "Who else hates us so much?"

"Or Russia," Walter rasped. "Those commie bastards have had it in for us since—"

"Let's not jump to conclusions," Julio soothed, wiping his hands on a towel, but he looked shaken himself. His hand strayed to the gold cross on a chain around his neck.

Then the news announced the third bomb.

No one said anything after that.

They watched the explosion filling the screen in dead silence.

All those people—tens of thousands, hundreds of thousands—gone in an instant.

How many thousands more were injured in the middle of that devastation? How could the hospitals and first responders handle that many dead and wounded?

They'd be overwhelmed. It wasn't just one bomb, but two. Three if you counted the one Chicago PD managed to diffuse.

There will be more. Logan felt it with a certainty he couldn't shake. The booze in his stomach turned to acid. Adrenaline iced through him.

"We should go," he said.

But no one heard him. They were glued to the news, too numb and shocked to respond.

He forced himself to stand. Part of him wanted to drown himself in whiskey until his mind was so pickled he didn't even remember his own name, let alone that hundreds of thousands of people had died—were dying—this very instant.

Another part of him burned with that survival instinct he'd never been able to fully shake, no matter how often he'd tried.

At least he had his trusty Glock 43 nestled in its concealed, inside-the-waistband holster at the small of his back.

Little good that would do against a bomb.

He needed to leave, to get out of the city, at least for a couple of days, until the danger had passed.

No city in America was safe right now.

He took another drink and set down a twenty beneath the bottle. His gaze swept the bar one last time and landed on the waitress he'd noticed before.

Average height, slim but strong, with a proud, defiant set to her shoulders. Strands of long auburn hair slipped from her messy ponytail. She wore sensible sneakers and a simple gray tank top with black cargo pants.

POINT OF IMPACT

There was something compelling about her features: sharp cheekbones, flinty eyes, but a softness around her jawline.

She looked tough, like the kind of girl who never backed down. The kind who'd sooner tell you to go to hell rather than take anyone's crap—especially a man.

The kind of girl he would have wanted to get to know back before everything happened, before he'd become a danger to himself and everyone around him.

The girl met his gaze. Her eyes were wide and scared, like everyone else's, but also grimly determined.

He'd seen her almost every day for three months since she'd started bussing tables. Suddenly, it seemed wrong that he'd never bothered to learn her name.

He opened his mouth to say something, maybe to warn her, but she didn't look like she needed to be warned. Her whole body was tense, one hand gripping a cell with whitened knuckles, the other curled into a fist.

She looked ready to run. Or fight.

Maybe he *was* paranoid, but at least he wasn't the only one. Maybe he should—

A flash of incandescent light brighter than the sun seared his eyes.

4

EDEN

ZERO HOUR MINUS EIGHT MINUTES...

Eden Sloane should have been working on her math homework for summer school. Instead, she perched on the wooden stool at the huge gray-and-white marble kitchen island, her drawing pad open and her artist-quality colored pencils arrayed in a rainbow-hued arc around her elbows.

Her notepad was filled with pages and pages of portraits and landscapes. She took practicing seriously; she dreamed of attending the Fine Arts Academy of Greater Miami.

But today, she was focused on another project. In painstaking detail, she'd drawn the hand figures for the alphabet in American Sign Language.

She wanted to share it with Dakota at their next supervised visit. Her sister didn't seem too interested in taking the class Mrs. Simpson had suggested, but maybe the visual pictures could help her get it.

Eden was a visual learner. Maybe Dakota was, too. Though at their last scheduled visit, Dakota told Eden she didn't need to learn sign language.

"We know how to communicate just fine," Dakota had huffed.

"You can hear me, and I know exactly what you're thinking just by looking at you. And if I don't, that's what your pad is for. It's worked just fine so far."

Dakota could be stubborn sometimes.

Eden sighed, finished sketching the spread pinkie and thumb of "Y", and gave the fingernails a sparkly plum-purple flourish.

The grandfather clock in the den dinged. The stainless-steel refrigerator whirred quietly. The walls creaked as the foundation settled. The big house made too many noises when she was alone.

Eden could hear just fine. It was speech that eluded her—that had eluded her since that day almost three years ago, her words stolen from her with the stab of a knife as swiftly and silently as her freedom, her choices, her family.

Instinctively, Eden touched the thick, ridged scar arcing across her throat. She didn't like thinking about that.

She glanced at the clock. It was just after 12:30 p.m. Her foster mother, Gabriella Ross, would be home from her tennis lessons in an hour; her foster father, Jorge, by six.

Eden went to summer classes in the mornings. She wasn't stupid, but school had never been much of a focus in her life before Ezra or the Rosses. This was just her way to catch up for high school, Mrs. Simpson had explained.

Either way, she'd rather draw.

She glanced at the Miami Herald newspaper clipping attached to the stainless-steel fridge with magnets. The article featured her first-place award in the Pérez Art Museum's annual youth art competition.

In the picture, she was hamming it for the camera, proudly holding up the framed drawing of an alligator lunging toward a wood stork escaping in mid-flight, wings thrashing as the gator's jaws closed over its pink feet.

Every time she looked at it, she swelled with happiness. She couldn't wait to tell Dakota. Dakota didn't like having their pictures taken, but surely she'd understand this time.

Her stomach growled, but she ignored it. She liked waiting for Gabrielle and sharing a late lunch. They always had family dinner together, too.

Her phone dinged. Not the iPhone her foster parents had bought for her fifteenth birthday a month ago, but her secret phone, the one she kept in the hidden compartment inside her backpack. The one only Dakota used.

Eden twisted around and fished it out of the backpack slung over the chair. She read the text, eyes widening in disbelief, then read it again.

Ezra right. Bombs. Find Shelter. I'm coming for you.

Eden had always thought Ezra was a little crazy in the head, with his paranoia and extreme safety precautions and prepping for years. But he'd saved them.

Was he right, after all?

Was the world really ending in fire and fury?

She didn't want to believe it. She wanted to finish her sign language project. She wanted to work on her math homework.

She wanted to listen contentedly while Gabriella turned up Spanish pop radio, dancing around the pristine kitchen while she unloaded take-out boxes onto fancy china plates—steaming General Tsao's chicken, vegetable lo mein and piles of white rice, and Eden's favorite honey chicken and broccoli.

She wanted to sit around the farm table and laugh and eat and sign the newest joke she'd learned at summer school.

Most of all, she longed to keep pretending she was a part of this family, where no one ever yelled or hurt her.

But she knew better than to dream when she needed to act.

She texted back: *Okay. At home.*

Her heart thumping against her ribs, she jumped off her seat, grabbed her notepad, a handful of pencils, and her phone, and looked around wildly.

The Rosses owned a sprawling five-thousand-square-foot, two-story stucco home. Like most Florida houses, it didn't have a basement.

Dakota hadn't said how much time she had. Eden had to assume immediate action. Better safe than sorry; that's what Ezra always said.

She closed her eyes. Think. *Think!* Where had Ezra said was the safest place?

She couldn't go to a basement. She had no time to find a big concrete office or apartment building. No underground bunkers to seek shelter inside.

Get to the middle. The center of a building is always safer than the exterior.

There was only one room in the house that didn't share an exterior wall or contain a window: the guest bathroom next to the guest bedroom on the first floor.

Eden sprinted out of the kitchen, through the formal living room, the expansive family room, and sunken den.

She lifted a cushion from the white leather sofa and lugged it down the long hallway lined with family photos—several with herself included—and into the bathroom.

She dropped the cushion on the ivory bathroom rug and faced the hallway for a second, her hand on the oiled bronze bathroom door handle.

This was crazy.

In less than an hour, Gabriella would come waltzing into the house with her warm, bustling energy, and everything would be normal and wonderful again.

If she found Eden cowering in the tub, her foster mom would think she really was crazy.

Maybe she'd think something was wrong with her, something worse than her mangled throat.

Maybe the Rosses would want to send her back to the Florida Department of Children and Families, back into the system.

She shuddered. What was she thinking? She didn't want to risk the good thing she had going. She was just starting to feel comfortable here.

Like she belonged.

Like maybe she had a family again.

Dakota was paranoid. Dakota always assumed the worst.

But no. Dakota was her sister. She was smart; she was prepared. She would never warn Eden of something so serious unless it was true.

Unless—

A brilliant white light flared down the hallway.

Eden couldn't see any windows from her vantage point, but it was like a giant spotlight beaming through every window of the house.

The light bouncing off the hallway walls was still harsh enough to make spots flare in front of her eyes.

Heart sputtering inside her chest, she slammed the bathroom door shut, whirled, and dove for the bathtub, seizing the large cushion as she went.

The bathroom was small. In two steps, she was in the tub, lying flat on her back, the cushion pulled over her head and torso —Dakota's flip phone gripped in one hand, her notepad pressed to her chest in the other.

By the time she realized she'd forgotten to count, a deafening thunder was already roaring over her, trembling the whole house in its primal fury.

5

MADDOX

ZERO HOUR MINUS FIVE MINUTES...

"I found them," Maddox Cage said into his phone.

"Both of them?" asked the deep baritone voice on the other end.

"As good as. Where Eden is, the other will be close." He didn't say her name. After what she'd done, the man on the other end of the line hated to hear her name.

"Have you laid eyes on her?"

"I visited her summer school this morning and waited until I saw her walk into the building with her foster mother."

"Tell me immediately when you have them." His voice went hard. "Both of them."

"I understand."

"And Maddox—don't delay. Get them now and get out of the city. Do you understand?"

A strange shiver went down his spine. "Yes, sir. Is there something—"

The line went dead.

Maddox ended the call and leaned forward in the back seat of the taxi to peer out the window. Traffic had stopped for a stoplight, a tourist bus blocking his view directly ahead.

Large several-story buildings of glass and concrete rose on either side of him. Palm trees flanked the wide boulevard. On his left, giant cranes clung to the half-constructed framework of a sleek, high-rise condo like mechanical spiders.

Pedestrians strolled past, some in business suits, many in Hawaiian shirts and Bermuda shorts, girls in crop tops and tiny shorts swaying their hips, all of them sweating in the early afternoon heat.

He turned his gaze away in disgust.

One of the many reasons why he despised the city. That and the singed stench of car exhaust, the constant stimulation of honking horns and roaring engines, chaotic crowds, and the bright lights and steel everywhere he looked.

He much preferred the peace of the natural world, the stillness and order in the vast rivers of grass he called home.

The traffic light seemed to go on forever. "How much longer?" he asked, restraining his anxiousness.

"A couple miles," said the taxi driver, a Haitian man with a full, bristling beard and konpa music playing low on his smartphone. "Fifteen minutes maybe in this mess."

Maddox Cage was close enough to smell victory. He could feel it like a buzzing beneath his skin.

They were both here.

He'd been hunting the girls off and on for almost three years now, his father growing more infuriated and impatient with every passing month.

He'd almost caught them in Everglades City two years ago, but they'd managed to elude him.

Dakota must have changed their names. Somehow, they'd simply disappeared.

But yesterday, his father, Solomon Cage, honorable brother of the Prophet, leader of the Shepherds of Mercy, had handed Maddox a folded slip of paper with a single address on it.

They never communicated via email or phone, unless it was a disposable burner cell. For the most part, they stayed off the internet, too. It was safer that way.

Paper could be disposed of. It didn't leave an electronic trail.

He did use the internet to search for his quarry, though. Constantly trolling through records both public and private, checking newspapers, hospitals, DMV databases, and arrest warrants.

Not a single hit in two years. Maddox had failed to find them...until two days ago. Scrolling quickly through the Miami Herald, like he did for dozens of regional papers, his eye snagged on a picture of a familiar beaming face.

He'd managed to discover them hiding in a city of half a million people.

He had found them—when they could've fled to Naples, Fort Myers, Marco Island, south to the Keys, or north to any of the hundreds of towns and cities in central and northern Florida.

He knew he had them both. Wherever Eden was, Dakota was certainly nearby.

He gave the name of the girl—Eden Sloane—and of the foster parents to his father. Within a day, he had the address in hand.

Maddox finally had a lead. He wasn't about to fail. Not this time.

Eden would return to her rightful place. And Dakota...Dakota would be brought back to face the consequences of her crimes.

Maddox Cage believed in justice. In judgment.

Now, finally, justice would be served. And he would be the one to serve it.

But first, he had a quick errand. His cousin, Rueben, had

asked him to pick up a package from the South Florida Container Terminal at the Port of Miami.

He didn't know what it was. He didn't need to know.

His father and cousin served the Prophet; so did he.

He sucked in his breath as the taxi entered the Port of Miami tunnel.

He clenched his hands on his lap until his nails dug into his calloused palms. His stomach roiled, the black bean tacos he'd grabbed at a cafe in Overtown settling uneasily.

He hated heights, but he despised this trapped, underwater feeling even more.

He was one hundred and twenty feet below the surface. He felt every foot of it like a ton of bricks collapsing against his chest, an immense pressure cutting off his breath, sending his heartbeat into a hammering cacophony in his ears.

His burner phone beeped. He pulled it out of his pocket. It was from an unidentified number, but Maddox knew who the sender was: his cousin, Reuben.

A text: *Plans changed. Forget the package. Get out now. It's coming.*

He squinted down at the phone, perplexed. Could Reuben mean what Maddox thought he did? Could it possibly be? The hairs on the back of his neck prickled.

What? he texted back.

He never got the chance to hit send.

A dazzling light blasted down the tunnel from behind him. It lit up the interior of the vehicle, blighting everything in his vision with a scorching brilliance.

"What the hell!" the taxi driver cried.

Maddox instinctively leaned over, his seat-belt digging into his stomach. He covered his head with his hands and squeezed his eyes shut against the brutal, blinding light.

It felt like staring straight at the sun.

"What was that?" shouted the driver. "What's happening—"

An earsplitting boom thundered through the tunnel, vibrating the air with its monstrous roar. Thousands of tons of concrete shuddered and heaved overhead.

He felt the taxi being lifted and flung through the air.

His seat-belt jerked against his lap and seared his neck as the vehicle slammed against the concrete wall of the tunnel.

Everything went black.

6
LOGAN
ZERO HOUR

"Don't look!" the waitress screamed. "Get down!"

Fear tore through him. Logan didn't think. He only reacted.

He squeezed his eyes shut and hurled himself away from the windows toward the booths. He lunged behind the closest one—thankfully empty—and squeezed his large frame beneath the table against the wall.

A tremendous heat blasted him, like an enormous oven opened inches from his entire body. Cowering, he flung his hands over his closed eyes.

A million blaring, high-voltage lights bored into his eyeballs like a drill, stunning and painful and endless.

Though it lasted only a second, it felt like an eternity—if it went on even an instant longer, his eyeballs would burst inside their sockets.

"One, two, three," the waitress chanted.

She scrambled in beside him. He heard and felt her, his eyes still shut, bright white light pulsing against his closed eyelids. He made room for her, pushing back as far against the wall as he could.

Screams and shrieks echoed all around them.

"I'm blind!"

"I can't see!"

"Help me!"

"Five, six, seven—" the waitress said.

Before he could ask what she was doing, a thunderous crack exploded with a great boom like the very sky was splitting open above them. An unearthly roar, mighty and shaking, tore through the Beer Shack.

Almost instantly, every glass pane exploded inward. A tremendous, howling wind with the force of a hurricane blasted them, jarring the concrete walls and ceiling. The floor heaved like a ship beneath him. The table shook and quivered, the booth at his back shuddering.

The flat-screen behind the bar fractured and clattered to the floor. Glass shattered and liquid splattered to the floor as shelves lined with alcohol bottles collapsed.

Great shudders thudded through the floor and walls, large objects toppling as if a giant's fists were smashing through buildings, breaking concrete and metal and steel.

A scream strained behind his clenched teeth. The entire building groaned, shivering violently, the walls snapping and popping.

A sharp crack sounded above him. Chunks of drywall and dust rained down on the table top above his head as if the roof itself was collapsing in on them.

Finally, the shaking stopped.

From out on the street came the horrific sounds of tires screeching, horns blasting, metal smashing against metal as cars slammed helplessly into each other, their drivers blinded.

Screams rent the air—hundreds, thousands of people screaming and shouting. Cries of pain and panic, of shock and terror.

The sounds seemed to come from far away. His ears were ringing.

Logan tried to open his aching eyes. There were only streaks of white. He blinked. Still just a fuzzy, painful whiteness.

He couldn't see.

"I'm blind," he mumbled, his mind frantically trying to comprehend what had just happened. He felt like his brain had just been shaken right out of his skull.

"Flash blindness," the waitress said.

He almost flinched at the nearness of her voice. He'd forgotten she was even there. He shied away, his hand instinctively going for his weapon. Without sight, he was vulnerable, completely helpless. "What?"

"You're not blind. It'll go away in a few minutes."

He felt her move away, heard her scrambling out from beneath the booth. "Be careful. There's glass everywhere."

He tried to wrap his mind around it. His heart jack-hammered against his ribs, but his thoughts came slow and sluggish.

Another nuclear bomb. It had to be. Nothing else made any sense.

A nuclear bomb had just detonated in downtown Miami.

He blinked and rubbed his eyes. Blinked again. White spots swirled and flickered across his eyelids. He could just make out the shadowy shape of the girl rising to her feet and brushing glass from her clothes.

Wetness leaked down his right cheek and neck. Blood dripped from several cuts. Several shards of glass were embedded in his skin. He felt for them gingerly and plucked them out one by one, ignoring the stings of pain. His hands trembled.

He shook his head, trying to clear the cobwebs.

One thing at a time. Focus. Think clearly.

But he couldn't seem to do that. His brain kept screaming nuclear bomb! again and again and again.

"Is it safe to come out?"

"Nothing is safe," the waitress said.

He couldn't think of a thing to say to that. He rubbed his eyes again, the white spots finally fading enough that he could see to clamber out from beneath the table.

He coughed, struggling to breathe, and raked his hand through his hair. Particles of dust drifted to the floor.

Thick gray dust swirled through the air. Debris and glass littered the tile. Most of the tables and booths near the window were broken and splintered like someone had taken an ax to them.

Only the two against the far wall—including the one he and the girl had sheltered beneath—were spared.

"Oh, hell." The waitress was looking behind them.

Logan turned to see zigzagging cracks spreading across the side walls flanking the hallway at the rear of the building. Above the hallway entrance glimmered a patch of gray, smoke-ridden sky.

The roof over the back section of the Beer Shack had partially collapsed. Great chunks of concrete and roof tumbled into the hallway that led to the bathrooms, storage, and staff room.

Ten more feet and the roof would've collapsed on top of him.

From the other side of the bar, someone moaned.

"What the hell was that?" a woman cried. "What happened?"

"A nuclear blast," the waitress said.

"No way," said a preppy white guy with his dirty-blond hair in a ponytail at the base of his neck. "It was an earthquake!"

"You an idiot? This is Florida, man."

"An earthquake happened in Tennessee, so what do you know?"

"A tornado," someone else said. "Like a hurricane of glass. That roaring sound—it was the most terrible thing I've ever heard."

"No quake. And no tornado, either. It was a nuke. Like on the news." Julio stood behind the bar, drenched in beer and alcohol from dozens of broken bottles, blood streaking his face. Amber and clear glass shards pierced his face, neck, arms, torso.

A piece the size of Logan's thumb jutted from the man's right thigh.

"You need medical attention," Logan said.

"Nah, I'm fine," Julio said, though his face was pale. "Just don't care for blood is all." He pointed a blood-stained finger. "Help her."

A blonde woman in her mid-forties slumped against one of the fallen bar stools beside a younger man with brown hair pulled back in a ratty ponytail. Logan recognized her as one of the regulars—Tamara Santos.

A three-foot-long metal rod had somehow punched through the shattered window, and now protruded from the woman's stomach. Her white-knuckled fingers clenched the shaft as red spread in a widening ring across her cream silk blouse.

"Help—me!" cried a heavy, bald Indian guy in his fifties. His pallor had gone ashen. He sucked in panicked, uneven breaths. The man had been thrown from his seat by the blast and slammed against the far wall.

He huddled on the floor amid the glass and debris, cradling his right arm to his chest. A white stab of bone poked from a bloody gash in his forearm.

A few feet away, old Walter leaned heavily against the bar, breathing hard and rubbing his rib cage. Blood dripped from several cuts on his wrinkled forehead. "I think I busted a rib, and I can't work my leg right. Call the paramedics!"

"They're not coming." The waitress scraped her hand across her face, a laceration on her forearm leaving a streak of blood behind. She stumbled to the broken windows. Glass jagged as teeth rimmed every frame. "No one is coming."

Logan followed her, picking his way through the debris: the tipped and broken bar stools, a fallen ceiling fan, one unbroken blade still spinning lazily.

More sounds from outside filtered through the ringing in his ears. Car alarms blaring. Screams and shrieks and desperate cries for help. The stench of gasoline and burning rubber filled his nostrils.

But it was the sight before him that stole his breath and iced his insides.

The mid-rise apartment building across the street was half caved in, as if a wrecking ball had struck its entire left side. Great chunks of brick and concrete had slid from the building and smashed into the asphalt.

A chunk the size of a small house had obliterated a car. It was only a mangled mess of metal now, the wheels barely visible beneath the onslaught of rubble.

Further down the street, a pile-up of at least thirty cars smoked and burned, the crumpled frames of trucks, vans, and cars barely recognizable.

A telephone pole had fallen across a capsized bus. A Starbucks blazed, flames leaping from the shattered windows.

People pulled themselves from burning cars, staggering, choking, screaming. Others slumped against the curb, bleeding, cradling injuries, staring blankly at the carnage around them.

A little Latino boy wept, his mother trying to comfort him.

Her dress was torn and bloodied. She only wore one sandal; one foot was bare, her nails painted a vivid teal.

Several men raced by, followed by a black couple tugging two middle-school-aged girls behind them, faces panic-stricken and smudged with dirt.

"Look," the waitress whispered, pointing at the sky.

Dreading what he would see, Logan slowly raised his eyes.

Above the screaming chaos, crashed cars and downed trees and shattered glass, above the apartment buildings and shopping complexes, rose a terror like he had never seen.

An immense black cloud boiled into the sky—blotting out the sun, blotting out everything.

7

DAKOTA

Dakota stared at the immense cloud as it boiled above downtown Miami, monstrous and raging, a violent orange-red mass almost a mile wide with a fiery blood-red core. The massive cloud punched up through the atmosphere, climbing and expanding at an astonishing rate, the air around it ionizing until the sky took on a savage glow.

The colossal cloud swelled with a terrible, violent swiftness until it seemed to blot out the whole horizon.

It continued to rise as if it would break through the sky itself.

Until that moment, it hadn't seemed completely real.

It was real now.

She desperately hoped Eden had obeyed her instructions, that she'd found a way to protect herself until Dakota could reach her.

"We've been nuked?" asked a pony-tailed guy kneeling over his injured girlfriend. "How is that possible?! I thought our silo missiles would shoot down anything headed our way!"

"They would." Dakota squinted, her eyes still slightly blurry. "But this is a groundburst. An airburst wouldn't have the stem of the mushroom touching the ground, and it would be lighter, white almost. Not like this."

"What does that mean?" Julio asked.

"It detonated on the ground." Her stomach clenched, acid burning the back of her throat. She took several slow, steadying breaths and wracked her brain to recall all the things Ezra had warned her about. "It's not a missile strike."

"What was that flash of light, then?" asked Walter, who was next to Ponytail, crouched on the floor over the blonde woman—Tamara—with the metal rod impaled through her stomach. "And that noise like a freight train?"

"A nuclear blast releases massive amounts of energy in the form of a giant fireball, a light and heat wave, a shockwave blast, and radiation," Dakota said.

She stared at the mushroom cloud rising from the earth—dark, heavy, and menacing.

"We must be far enough from ground zero to have missed the fireball and the worst of the light wave. The thermal heat wave was probably blocked by the large apartment buildings across the street or other buildings along its path."

"How do you know?" Ponytail blinked at her rapidly. He was still partially blind.

"We'd have second- and third-degree burns," she said simply. "Or we'd be dead."

"How far are we from the actual blast?" Logan asked.

She'd had the presence of mind to count the seconds between the light wave and the shockwave, which worked much like thunder and lightning. Though she wasn't positive if she'd started counting fast enough.

"The shockwave travels nearly a thousand feet a second, while the light wave is almost instantaneous," she explained hurriedly. "By counting the seconds between them, you get a rough idea of your distance from the blast. I counted seven seconds, but I probably missed a second in the beginning. So about a mile and a half from ground zero, give or take."

"So we're safe here," Walter said.

"I didn't say that." She glanced at her analog watch, the one Ezra bought her for her seventeenth birthday over two-and-a-half years ago.

12:40 p.m. The bomb had exploded at 12:38. Two minutes had already passed. "We need—"

"Where did the bomb hit?" the bald guy interrupted.

"The point of impact must be somewhere downtown," Dakota said. "There's no way to know for certain yet."

Julio sucked in his breath as he gingerly tugged a large amber shard from his thigh. Blood darkened his jeans.

"You okay?" Dakota strode across the glass-strewn floor and handed Julio her apron over the bar. He was bleeding heavily. "There are more clean hand towels stacked beneath the sink."

Julio pulled out a smaller shard from his forearm with a wince. "Just a prick."

"We have to get in there and help those people!" said Jesse Peretti, the full-bearded Jewish accountant slumped at the end of the bar.

His long beard was bloodied, pieces of glass clinging to the graying bristles, a gruesome purple knot the size of an egg forming on his right temple. He swayed as he stood. He'd suffered a concussion, at least. "My daughter works on Brickell Key—"

Dakota shook her head. Pity welled inside her, but she didn't know how to help him other than to speak the truth, no matter how harsh it was. "Everything located within the epicenter of that fireball—within a half-mile radius at least—it's all gone."

They stared at her, shocked numb.

"We're talking temperatures of 300,000 degrees Celsius, fifty times hotter than the surface of the sun. The intensity of the thermal blast is hot enough to ignite birds in midair and liquify steel. It instantly vaporizes everything—buildings, cars, glass, asphalt. People."

For several seconds, no one spoke. The horror was too much for anyone to comprehend. Tens of thousands of people, all going about their normal, boring, pedestrian lives not five minutes ago—suddenly gone in the blink of an eye.

"At least we're safe here." Tears watered Ponytail's red-rimmed eyes. "We can wait until the firefighters and paramedics come for us."

Julio jerked out another glass chunk and pressed a towel to the wound. "Are you crazy, man? Don't you know anything about nukes? Remember Hiroshima?"

The guy stared at him blankly.

"What goes up must come down," Dakota said.

Logan rubbed the stubble along his jaw. "Fallout."

"I heard that was just a myth," Ponytail whined, like if he believed it strongly enough, he could make it true.

"If the fireball explodes in the air, like with a nuke, fallout is present but minimal," Dakota said, remembering one of Ezra's frequent lectures. "When it detonates on the ground, all the vaporized soil and debris get pulled up into the cloud. As the cloud travels downwind, the radioactive material cools and falls, creating a large swath of fallout and contaminating everything it touches."

"We need to get out of here." Logan turned to her. "What do you suggest?"

"Time, distance, and shielding," she muttered.

"What?"

"Three ways to get safe. We're within the radius for some

prompt radiation exposure, but a mile and a half out, it should be minimal."

"Okay, then we're fine—" Ponytail started.

"No, we're not. Which direction is the wind?"

Logan glanced out the windows at the row of palm trees across the street. "The wind is blowing north, I think. Toward us."

She felt dizzy, sick to her stomach. "If we're right and ground zero is south of us, then we're directly downwind."

"What does that mean?" Ponytail asked.

"A southerly wind—blowing south to north—will bring the worst of the fallout right to us. That's enough radiation to start destroying your internal organs within hours. It'll kill you in days."

"Okay," Julio said, his mouth tightening like he was struggling to keep himself calm. "What do we do?"

She fought to keep her own frantic panic under control. Panicking now could mean death. Only clear thinking and a plan would keep them alive.

"How long do we have?" Logan asked tersely.

She checked. 12:41 p.m. Three minutes had already passed.

When she spoke, her throat was raw. "The radioactive debris starts falling back to the ground about ten minutes after impact. We only have seven minutes to find shelter."

8
DAKOTA

"We can't do anything about time or distance. We need shielding," Dakota said. "We need a thick, dense barrier, and fast." She gestured at the shattered windows, the exposed air all around them. "This place won't cut it."

Bald Guy lurched to his feet, clutching his broken arm to his chest. "You said distance. My car's at the curb. I'm driving and getting as far from that bomb as possible!"

"If your car even works," Dakota said. "You see all these car wrecks? What about rubble? What're you gonna do when the roads are clogged and you're trapped out in the open? Your tin can of a car won't protect you once the radiation falls."

Bald Guy grimaced in pain and started to protest, but Logan shut him down with a sharp look. "What will protect us?" Logan asked.

"We need to get as much mass as possible between us and the radiation. The best shelter is the middle of a large building, or better yet, a basement underground."

"Thanks a lot, Florida water table," Walter grumbled.

"What about the huge office complex across from us?" Logan asked. "It's twelve stories."

Dakota glanced out the window at the shiny new building designed with huge panes of glass on every floor—every pane exploded in the blast. The left end sagged dangerously. A section at the top had collapsed.

"It's too damaged and unstable. Plus, an office building won't have enough food or water for a bunch of people to survive for a week."

"A week?" Tamara wheezed. "Are you insane?"

"There's the Showtime cinema," Julio said, ignoring her. "No windows in the auditoriums, thick cement block construction. Other stores on either side of it; plus there's a restaurant above it on the second-story promenade. That helps, right?"

"They have a concession counter," Walter said. "Lots of snacks and water bottles."

Logan moved toward the doorway, already scanning the street outside the bar. "It's in that shopping center three blocks from here. We can be there in a few minutes."

Dakota nodded. It was as perfect as they were going to get. They didn't have time to consider any other options, and they'd wasted too many precious seconds already. Ezra had taught her better than this. "Let's go!"

Bald Guy pulled out his car keys with his unwounded hand. "There's no way in hell I'm staying someplace directly in the path of radioactive fallout." He stumbled through the shattered glass door, not even bothering to open the frame.

"I'm with him." Ponytail leapt to his feet, already palming his keys. "I'm getting as far away as fast as I can. You guys are crazy to listen to her. What does she know? She's just a waitress."

"Dakota knows plenty," Julio snapped with uncharacteristic sharpness. "She's got a good head on her shoulders. I trust her."

Dakota flashed Julio a tight, grateful smile. He'd always been kind to her. And fair. "It's fine. If he wants to be an idiot, let him be an idiot."

"Raphael! Don't leave me!" Tamara raised her hand weakly, grasping for her boyfriend.

"You'll be fine. I'll meet you at the hospital." Raphael barely squeezed her hand before striding through the door after the first guy. He never even glanced back.

"He always was an asshole," Tamara muttered, wincing.

Logan shook his head in disgust. "They made their choice. We need to go."

Julio moved gingerly around the corner of the bar. "Radioactive waste is about to fall on our heads. We have to go, now. Tamara, we can try to carry you. Let's get you up."

Jesse rubbed the purple knot on his forehead. He righted a bar stool and sank onto it. "It's safer to stay here and wait for an ambulance and the police."

"There's no time," Dakota warned. "We only have a few minutes."

Tamara shook her head stubbornly. Her eyelids fluttered. Her pallor was ashen from the loss of blood. "I'm staying right here and waiting for the paramedics."

"No paramedics are coming!" Dakota bit back her frustration. "Don't you get it? No one's coming. Not for a long time."

But they wouldn't move.

Dakota wasn't a sociopath. She didn't want to leave them. But she wasn't going to get killed for anyone too stubborn to see the truth, either.

"Count me in," Walter rasped. He tried to push himself off the bar counter, but his right leg twisted beneath him, and he stumbled. "There's no way I'm stayin' behind and lettin' y'all have all the fun."

Julio came around the bar and grabbed his arm. "We'll help you. Don't worry."

For a heartbeat, Dakota looked longingly back at the rear of the bar, at the collapsed beams and slab of roof blocking the hallway to the staff room.

Her bug out bag was in there. And her XD9. She could make it without the contents of the bag, but the gun...

Two of the fallen beams shifted, rubbing against each other with a groaning, grinding sound. A spray of dust and rubble snowed down on several nearby tables.

"We've got to go now!" Logan said.

She knew he was right. She set her jaw and strode to the shattered doorway. "Anyone who doesn't want to die of radiation, come with me."

9
LOGAN

Logan wrapped his arm around Walter's frail shoulders and helped him hobble along. Dakota jogged beside him, panting, with Julio just behind them.

A blast of humidity struck them as they left the bar. Logan's pits and lower back were instantly damp.

The street was in chaos. Smoke clouded the air, everything covered in a film of dust. Fires blazed everywhere.

They raced along the sidewalk, past downed telephone poles and street lights, palm trees sheared and broken. In several places, they were forced to move into the street to avoid piles of smoking rubble from partially collapsed storefronts.

In the street, cars were flung about, their metal frames crushed and twisted, dozens toppled on their sides. A shiny apple-red Ford Mustang lay upside down, the roof crumpled, steam hissing out from the twisted hood, wheels still spinning.

A Ford F150 had plunged into a Dunkin' Donuts storefront, great chunks of the walls and ceiling of the structure collapsed around it.

People moved around him, gasping, covering their mouths,

crying out in terror. Some were bruised and battered, others bleeding. They staggered blindly into the street, dazed and bewildered.

Others sank to the curbs, clutching at their cuts and bruises and broken bones in stunned disbelief.

"I can't see!" someone screamed.

"My husband! He needs help!"

"My eyes...there's something wrong with my eyes..."

"Help us, please!"

They sounded distant and remote; he hardly heard them through the roaring in his own ears. His legs felt heavy as lead, his breathing ragged.

Sweat already soaked his underarms, dampened his hairline, and dripped into his eyes—sweat from the heat, but also the kind he knew so well—the sour sweat of fear.

"Radiation!" Dakota yelled at the people they passed. "Seek shelter!"

A handful of people remained in their cars, scowling and cursing, trying unsuccessfully to start them. At the curb, a woman sat in a silver Tesla, frozen with her hands on the wheel, unmoving, unblinking, her eyes wide and blank with shock. No cars were working, not even the ones undamaged from the multiple pile-ups.

"Something's wrong with my phone!" Julio panted. He held it as he ran, punching desperately at the screen. "I can't call my wife!"

"An EMP," Logan said as the realization hit him. He hadn't even thought about it, but of course, it made sense. He'd seen a documentary about it on Netflix.

"What?" Walter said. "You just said it was a nuclear blast—"

"It is." Logan sucked in a mouthful of muggy, smoky air. He kept himself fit in the boxing ring, but the old man was heavier than he looked. "The blast radiates an electromagnetic pulse that disrupts or destroys all electronics and the electrical grid—cell towers, telecommunication switches, radar, phones, computers, cars."

"Mother Mary and Joseph," Julio gasped. "Across the whole city?"

"No." Dakota slowed down as she edged around a tangle of fallen, sparking power lines. "Only within a three-to-five-mile radius from ground zero."

He wiped at his stinging eyes. The stench of burning things—plastic, metal, flesh—overwhelmed his senses.

A fire engulfing a four-story office building completely blocked the road ahead of them, forcing them to backtrack and find a side street.

The sound of crying drew his gaze.

On their right, across the street, the roof of a designer clothing shop had caved in. A small shape huddled against the trunk of a downed palm tree. A girl of nine or ten with straggly, dirty-blonde hair.

She was dressed in denim shorts and a too-small purple Disney princess shirt. Her pink-framed glasses were set crookedly on her tear-streaked, sooty face.

The girl stared at them in mute terror. A blue stain dripped down the front of her shirt, across the blonde princess's face. More of it puddled on the ground at her feet, along with a small, flat stick.

A Popsicle. She was just a kid happily licking a Popsicle. And then the bomb went off.

Logan's gut twisted. A face flashed in his mind, unbidden, unwanted—small and round, large pleading eyes black as prayer beads, desperate and full of terror. He pushed the thought down deep.

Ahead of him, Dakota slowed, wiped sweat from her brow, and held out her hand to the girl. "Radiation's coming. It can kill you. Come with us to the movie theater."

The girl shook her head. "My mom's in there." She gestured behind her plaintively. "I keep calling her, but she won't come out."

Logan glanced at the caved-in shop. The collapsed roof listed dangerously. It was a death trap.

Even if the woman was still alive, she was likely gravely injured. They didn't have the time, the knowledge, or the tools to safely rescue her.

Dakota hissed out a frustrated breath. She glanced at her watch then down the street toward the shopping plaza. "Come on."

"I—I can't."

"You have to worry about yourself now," Julio said, trying to reason with the girl. "We can come back for your mom later."

The little girl pushed out her lower lip, fighting back sobs, and shook her head. "She told me to stay with her, no matter what."

Julio reached for her hand. "Come on, honey—"

The girl shrank back with a terrified squeal.

Julio froze.

"What should we do?" he asked uncertainly.

"Leave her," Walter growled. "We don't got the time for heroism."

Logan and Dakota exchanged strained glances.

It wasn't his business. There were people suffering and dying all over the city. What was one more kid? She wasn't their responsibility. She certainly wasn't his.

Overhead, the sky darkened.

"Fallout's coming," Dakota warned. "It's been seven minutes."

He fought his desire to leave them all behind and just run for his own self-preservation. It wasn't a feeling he'd been acquainted with recently. But it was still there—the innate, instinctive desire to survive at all cost.

"Look!" Logan pointed down the street. "The theater's right there. We need to go!"

Something like disappointment shadowed her face for the briefest moment. She shook her head, turning away from Logan, and muttered a curse.

She grabbed the girl's upper arms, yanked her up, and shook her, hard. "If you wanna live, you've got to run!"

Stunned, the girl stared up at her, mouth hanging open, her glasses nearly falling off.

Dakota didn't bother with an answer. She broke into a sprint, still grasping the girl by her wrist in an iron grip. The girl stumbled, crying out, but the waitress ignored her and jerked her back to her feet.

She took off down the street, dragging the weeping girl behind her.

"What're you waiting for?" Walter growled in Logan's ear.

They ran.

10

DAKOTA

Dakota raced across the parking lot, pulling the girl behind her, her lungs burning, her heart hammering in her throat.

She hadn't wanted to shake the girl so hard, but it was the only thing she knew to do to snap the kid out of her fugue. Maybe there were alternatives, but they all would've taken precious seconds they didn't have.

At least the girl would live.

As it was, time was already running out. The hot air swirled around her, the rapidly blackening sky bearing down on them all as they ran.

They had only minutes until it was toxic. What if it was already contaminated, invisible poisons sinking deep into her exposed skin?

She shook the fear off like a dog shaking itself dry. It wouldn't do anything but bring on debilitating panic. To survive, she had to *think.*

Showtime 14, the fourteen-theater cinema, was situated in the center of a U-shaped, two-story shopping center between an Old Navy, a Dollar Tree, Walgreens, and various boutiques and restaurants. Broken glass littered the gaping windows and doors, but the massive stucco and concrete-block building looked solid enough.

A group of teen boys stood in a clump in the parking lot, gazing up at the mushroom cloud invading the sky with open mouths.

"Get inside!" Logan shouted at them.

Dakota pulled the girl slipping and stumbling across the parking lot, ignoring her wails. "Don't fall, or you'll cut yourself on all the glass."

The girl straightened and somehow managed to avoid tripping until they reached the cinema. Inside, the foyer was cloaked in shadows, the only light streaming in through the front windows.

Dakota looked at her watch. 12:46 p.m. Eight minutes.

A few dozen people milled about near the concessions bar, most frowning down at their non-working phones or gesturing toward the shattered windows, confusion and trepidation on their faces.

Several families trickled out from various auditoriums, probably because the power had switched off halfway through their film.

They all stared as Dakota and the others rushed in, disheveled and bleeding, dragging a weeping, panic-stricken child with them.

"A nuclear bomb just detonated!" Dakota shouted. "Radioactive fallout is about to rain down. Get away from the windows and doors!"

Some people gasped and moved back instinctively, pulling their children with them.

A skinny man wearing a Marlins cap with a round basketball gut shook his useless phone. "Where did you hear that? We can't even turn the damn thing on! Power's broken."

"We saw it," Logan said steadily. "If you went outside, you'd see the mushroom cloud for yourselves. But I highly recommend you restrain yourself. One look could cost you a hell of a cancer diagnosis six months from now."

Marlins Cap balked. "You're talking nonsense. That's crazy."

"We saw it too!" one of the teen boys exclaimed from behind them. "It was epic!"

"Epically terrifying," another boy mumbled, sounding a bit sick.

Gasps and mutters filled the room. Strangers exchanged appalled, disbelieving looks. A woman covered her young daughter's ears.

Dakota didn't have time for another philosophical discussion with skeptics and idiots. There was too much to do to stay alive.

She looked down at the girl and released her hand. "See the concession counter over there? If you can sit here quietly without moving, you can eat whatever you want. Deal?"

The girl sank down to the floor and crossed her skinny legs. She wiped her nose with the back of her arm and hugged her arms to her chest, still trembling, but finally, she nodded.

One problem taken care of, for the moment.

Dakota turned to Julio, Walter, and Logan. "Go behind the counter and grab all the packaged snacks you can. Get the plastic buckets for the popcorn. We'll need them for water. As many as you can!"

"You can't do that!" A scrawny, pimply-faced redhead squeaked from behind the counter, an "assistant manager" badge pinned to his blue staff shirt. "That's stealing!"

"I prefer to call it borrowing," Logan said.

"You're crazy!" the kid sputtered. "I'm calling the police!"

"Go for it." But when Logan strode around the counter, the kid backed up, raising his hands, palms out, shaking his head.

Logan cut an imposing figure. He was strong and fit. She

could tell he knew his way around a fight just by the confident, languid way he moved, the alert wariness in his gaze. She tucked that bit of information away.

It might come in useful later.

Logan ignored the kid and reached beneath the counter for a stack of yellow-striped plastic buckets. Julio reached carefully into the broken display cases and gathered boxes of Whoppers, Nerds, Reese's Pieces, and Sweet Tarts.

"What do you think you're doing?" A short, burly man barely as tall as Dakota stalked over. He punched a fat finger at his own chest. "This is *my* theater."

"We're trying to save as many lives as possible, including yours," Julio said diplomatically, with a level of patience Dakota would never obtain.

"You're out of your mind!" the manager growled. "You're a danger to the patrons!"

"It's the bomb that's the danger, man," one of the teen boys said. "Get a grip."

The manager glared at him, his broad face purpling. "If you haven't paid for a ticket, then you've got no business being here!"

Frustration clawed at her. Dakota fought to keep her voice steady. "We're not leaving."

The manager puffed out his chest aggressively and jutted his fleshy chin. "I don't care where you go, but it won't be on my property. I insist you leave immediately. Get out!"

11
DAKOTA

Dakota opened her mouth to rip the asshat a new one.

Logan stepped forward. His hands were loose at his sides, but the muscles beneath his tattoos tensed and bulged.

Just his presence was intimidating, and he knew it.

The manager paled.

"We're not going anywhere," Logan said in a low, dangerous voice.

Julio pulled several twenties out of his jeans pocket and held them out to the manager. A few speckles of blood stained the wrinkled bills. "Consider that a deposit on a later payment. I'm no thief. I'll pay whatever bill you'd like. For all of us."

"If you think—" the manager started.

"Take the money," Logan growled.

The man's face was so red it looked about to explode. He glared up at Logan, who stared icily back. He opened his mouth to speak something inhospitable.

Logan took another step forward. He towered over the short, squat man.

The manager's features contorted at some inner battle

between self-preservation and oversized ego. Finally, his shoulders sagged in capitulation. He seemed to understand that he didn't have a choice in the matter.

At least the money was a way to salvage his wounded pride.

He snatched the cash with the tips of his fingers. "This is only the down payment!"

"I'm good for it," Julio said wearily. "Don't worry."

The manager scowled at the droplets of blood landing on the burgundy carpet at Julio's feet. His beady eyes flicked to Logan. Wisely, he said nothing.

She'd had enough. "There's no time for this crap!" she shouted. "Don't you people get it?"

Everyone fell silent, staring at her in astonishment, all of them still expecting the old rules of polite and civilized behavior to apply.

But that world was gone.

It had blown itself into smithereens eight minutes ago.

"Radioactive fallout is coming right now! The bomb is real. Sheltering in place is the safest thing to do. And we need to get to that shelter in the next minute before the radiation starts eating you from the inside out!"

"Even *if* it's true, there's no way we're staying here," Marlins Cap growled. He gripped his wife's arm. "It looks fine out there. We're getting out while we still can."

The wife, a mousy little thing, glanced back at Dakota as the man hauled her out, alarm etched across her thin face. But she allowed herself to be led away.

"You're making a mistake!" Dakota called after them. She gritted her teeth, willing the anger down. She'd seen plenty of women like that before—cowed, docile, obedient to a fault.

It made her want to punch something.

More people followed their lead. Three other families moved

toward the front doors along with them. Dozens streamed out into the darkening parking lot, desperate to find their families, to get home—a place that sounded safe, but was anything but.

"I believe you." A curly-haired Hispanic woman dressed in a purple flowered maxi dress clutched her purse to her chest, her expression stricken. "I saw the windows blow out. I felt the whole building shake. Why else aren't our phones working?"

The woman's gaze darted to the shattered windows and back to Dakota. "But my daughter is at her ballet class less than a mile from here. I don't care what's coming for me. I'm not leaving her."

Dakota understood that desperation better than anyone. She felt it clawing up her throat, tightening her chest, roaring in her ears. All she wanted to do was get to Eden.

But if she left now, she might be dead before she even got there. She couldn't give in to her fear. Fear made people stupid, Ezra always said. And stupid got people killed. She had to be smart.

She could already see the woman wasn't going to change her mind, but she tried anyway. "Maybe your daughter found shelter where she is. If you wait even several hours, the radiation lessens dramatically."

The woman shook her head.

"In two hours, it'll be half of what it is right now. In seven hours, seven times less. You might make it—"

"I'm driving to her right now. She needs me."

"Your car won't start because of the EMP. Even if it does, the debris will block your way."

The woman's mouth tightened in a straight, bloodless line. "I'll walk if I have to. It's a risk, but so is staying here."

Dakota gave a resigned sigh. "The wind is blowing the fallout north. For now. But it could change direction. Just make sure you head perpendicular to the wind, okay? Get your daughter and get as far away as you can. Prompt radiation will be everywhere within a few miles of ground zero. But the fallout carried by the wind can settle radioactive particles sixty or more miles away."

The woman grasped Dakota's hand and squeezed. "Thank you."

Dakota didn't have time to watch her go.

She checked her watch. 12:46. Nine minutes.

She turned to the worker behind the ticket booth, a tall, willowy black girl nervously biting her nails, her dead phone in her other hand. Her name tag read "Mishayla Harris."

"Do you have any flashlights? With the power out and no windows, we need to be able to see inside the theater."

"We have five flashlights in the storage room for emergencies." The girl stopped chewing her nails long enough to run her hand over her thick, wild mane of tight coils skimming the tops of her shoulders.

She slanted her eyes warily at the strangely darkening sky outside. "Is it really a nuclear attack? Bombs and everything? I just —it doesn't seem real."

"Yeah, it's real. Bring me the flashlights," Dakota said. "Which auditorium is the most centered in the middle of the building?"

"Number seven. We were showing the newest Mission Impossible film—"

"Great." She raised her voice so everyone could hear. "Anyone who's staying, grab as much food and bottles of water as you can and meet in auditorium seven ASAP."

Mishayla glanced at the bloody cuts marring Julio's arms, face, and torso, and Walter's pained hobble. "We've got a first aid kit, too. I can help. I'm in nursing school."

"Perfect. Bring everything you can to the auditorium."

Mishayla hurried off toward an unmarked door behind the ticket counter.

Loaded with stacks of empty popcorn buckets and a pile of packaged candies, cookies, and chips, Logan and Julio headed down the wide hallway.

Walter limped along with the handful of people who hadn't left, their arms filled with packaged waters and juice bottles.

The manager stalked after them, glowering, trailed by the red-haired assistant manager. They both looked like they'd swallowed something sour and couldn't wait to spit it out.

Julio glanced back at her, questioning. "You're coming, right?" He was a thoughtful boss like that. A good guy.

She waved him on. "Take the girl, would you? I'm right behind you."

Turning toward the girl, Julio held out a snack-size bag of Oreos and gave her a kind, disarming smile. "Come on, honey."

She climbed unsteadily to her feet, her expression terrified, but she followed him down the darkened hallway with the others.

Dakota checked her watch one last time. 12:48. Eleven minutes.

She paused for a moment at the ticket booth, hesitating, her gaze drawn to the shattered windows a few dozen yards away.

She couldn't see the mushroom cloud this far inside the building, only the expanse of parking lot and a low sliver of sky behind a big box store.

The sky was dark as if before a storm, the air stained a hazy, sour yellow. Small dust-like particles drifted down like snow.

The fallout.

It was real.

The bomb was real.

How many thousands had just been vaporized? How many were wounded and dying, crushed beneath crumbling buildings or burned beyond recognition? How many cities? Five? Ten? More?

How many years would it take the country to recover? Would they ever recover from something as horrific as this?

Nothing would ever be the same.

She swallowed a silent scream. She couldn't let herself fall apart. She was the strong one; she was the one who kept everything together.

She could still do that. She could still protect Eden and find them a way out of this hell.

Was Maddox out there somewhere, still alive in the chaos? She hoped he was dead. She didn't care if it made her a terrible person. His death would be the only good thing about the apocalypse.

Her sister was out there, too. Hiding and scared, maybe all alone, maybe injured, but alive. She had to believe Eden was alive.

Dakota had rescued her once. She would do it again.

As soon as it was safe enough, maybe even before—the very minute she could escape without dooming herself to death—she was going out, out into the ruined city, and she was finding Eden.

12
DAKOTA

Mishayla brought the flashlights into the darkened theater, pitch-black but for the dim emergency lighting along the floor. Dakota let her keep one, took one for herself, and handed the others to Logan, Julio, and the manager, who'd reluctantly provided his name: Gary Schmidt.

"Don't make me regret this," she said as she pressed the handle into his fleshy palm.

Schmidt flicked it on and scowled at her. "You don't get to decide. Those are my flashlights. All of them."

Dakota was about to say something nasty when Julio stepped up beside her. "We can't express our appreciation enough for your generosity." His voice was calm and sincere, without a hint of sarcasm.

She glared at him, but he continued before she could interject. "When this is all over, I'm sure the news channels will love to cover stories of local businesses coming to the community's rescue. It'll be great for business."

Schmidt let out a huff. "It better be."

"Where do you want the food?" Walter asked from the front near the screen.

"Right there is fine," Dakota said. She didn't care about being in charge, but she'd do the job if she had to.

"And just who will be in charge of that?" Schmidt whined.

"Thanks, man." Julio slapped his back with a warm grin. "We really appreciate you volunteering."

Schmidt straightened his rounded shoulders. "Well, someone around here has to know what they're doing."

Julio winked at her. She just shook her head and turned away. Julio had a gift for smoothing bruised egos.

Dakota didn't care to even try.

She scanned the auditorium with the flashlight—about a hundred plush recliner seats, walls painted some dark color she couldn't discern, carpet a muted burgundy.

The little girl they'd rescued slumped in one of the oversized chairs, her legs pulled up beneath her as she nibbled on her bag of Oreos. She'd told them her name was Piper.

Fourteen other people huddled in clusters in the main aisle between the seats closest to the screen and the rest of them. Fifteen total, including two of the teen boys.

No, there were seventeen. A woman and a child sat amid the empty seats about halfway up.

The woman scowled down at them.

Dakota ignored her. What was she missing? What did they still need to survive the next several days?

She stared up at the ceiling, imagining the fallout descending on the roof above them. "Are you running a generator? We need to turn off the HVAC unit so it doesn't draw in radioactive particles from outside, just in case the power comes back online."

"It's an emergency generator, but it'll get hot—" Schmidt started.

She had no patience left for fools. "Just do it!"

Schmidt huffed but snapped his fingers at the assistant manager, who scurried off to obey.

Dakota closed her eyes, sending her mind back to that scarred wooden kitchen table, the warmth of the kerosene lamp, Ezra's wizened face and crinkling eyes, the way he would frown intently and jab at the table with his index finger when he wanted them to really listen.

There were five critical elements for survival: shelter, food, water, protection, and a plan. They had the shelter and some food. Now they had to work on the rest.

She opened her eyes, and her gaze fell on the popcorn buckets. "We need to fill them all up with water, as much as we can. The water lines could break or turn off at any time."

"What about contamination?" Julio asked. "Isn't that a danger?"

"It's possible but not likely. And not this soon."

She turned to look at the huddled group of strangers, keeping her flashlight down to keep from blinding anyone. "I'm not sure if we got here in time. We were probably exposed for a minute, maybe two.

"Other than the really high levels of fallout, radiation is invisible. You won't be able to see it or feel it, but it sticks to your skin and hair, your clothes, your shoes, everything. The longer it stays on you, the more damage it does.

"We need to go to the bathrooms and wash ourselves thoroughly. Take every piece of clothing off and scrub your body with soap and water. Make sure you wash your face—get your eyebrows and eyelashes, too.

"Then wash your hair. It's not like we have conditioners here, but they bind radioactive material to hair protein. Not a good idea. So only use soap and water.

"After you're clean, scrub every article of clothing you're wearing, inside and out. "It'd be best if we could bag and discard our clothes, but unless we feel like starting a nudist colony, I don't think that's a viable option."

Logan snorted.

"What if we scrub everything really well?" Piper squeaked with an appalled expression. "With lots of extra soap?"

Julio gave her a warm smile. "Good plan, kid."

Dakota swiveled her flashlight at Mishayla. "Will you lead us to the closest bathrooms in the center of the building, away from windows and exit doors?"

"Of course. There's a set of bathrooms one auditorium over."

"This seems a bit extreme," Schmidt said, puffing out his chest to make himself seem more imposing. "We hardly need to scare the children present with fear-mongering paranoia."

Dakota knew his kind. It didn't matter that she'd just met him. She knew people like him, from the priggish social worker Mrs. Simpson to her last smugly self-righteous foster parent.

And the ones from before, the people she no longer allowed herself to think about.

She wasn't going to waste her time or anyone else's trying to convince someone dead-set against logic. "We're doing it. You're free to make your own choices.

"For everybody else, after you wash yourself and your clothes, clean and fill every single bucket. We need a gallon of water a day per person for drinking and washing up. The water supply could shut down at any time."

13
DAKOTA

Dakota stuck her flashlight between her teeth, seized about fifty of the buckets, and strode down the hallway without a backward glance. "Piper, come with me."

Once in the bathroom, she set her flashlight on top of the blow dryer and angled it at the row of five sinks. The walls glimmered with white subway tile, the floors large gray asymmetrical squares.

She sighed with relief when she switched on the faucets, and sweet, sweet water rushed out.

Four women and two girls followed her into the bathroom, including Piper. She kept close to Dakota, hugging herself, the half-eaten Oreos bag clutched in one small fist.

A plump, curvy Middle Eastern woman in her mid-thirties stepped forward first, gracefully unbuttoning a saffron-yellow silk blouse and slipping out of a fitted charcoal skirt.

"Don't be shy," she said. She was pretty, with velvety light brown skin, high cheekbones, and a slightly upturned nose. She wore a beautiful, silken cornflower blue hijab.

Mishayla ripped off her uniform with a tight grin. She thrust out her hand. "Always disliked this thing, anyway. I'm Mishayla, by the way. My friends call me Shay."

The woman shook Shay's hand. "I'm Rasha. My husband Miles and I are supposed to be on vacation, visiting my mom but staying on South Beach. We flew in from Atlanta on Sunday.

"Miles got a sunburn and, well, we thought an afternoon movie would give his skin a break." She shrugged helplessly as she removed her hijab. "Now, here we are."

"Zamira," said a thin, older Cuban woman in her seventies, her entire face crinkling as she attempted a smile. "This is my granddaughter, Isabel. I watch her during the summer while her parents work."

She clasped the hand of a teenage girl around thirteen. Her head was lowered, her long black hair covering her face as she sniffled and wept quietly.

"I'm Dakota." Dakota gestured at the little girl beside her. "And this is Piper. We need to hurry."

Zamira pulled gently on her granddaughter, leading her to the sinks. She turned and gestured at Piper. "Come now, dears, let's get this done."

The women undressed quickly, stuffing their shirts and jeans and bras into the sinks and scrubbing themselves with soap-drenched paper towels.

Zamira washed Isabel, who stood limply, shivering and weeping. The girl was probably in shock.

Zamira gave Piper encouraging smiles until she tentatively stepped forward, though she took off her own clothes and washed herself.

Dakota watched the three of them for a moment. Zamira was a kind, grandmotherly woman. She reminded her of Sister Rosemarie, one of the only women who'd shown her true compassion in the compound. She knew Zamira would watch out for Piper.

She offered to help Zamira finish washing Isabel and Piper's hair.

"You should take care of yourself," Zamira said. "We're fine." But Zamira's hands were trembling. She was shivering from the cold, and she hadn't even cleaned herself yet.

"Let me help you," Dakota insisted, sharper than she intended.

But Zamira only smiled, her eyes nearly disappearing in a net of wrinkles. "I can see you're a girl used to getting her way."

"Don't I wish," Dakota muttered.

"What about you?" Piper asked.

Dakota just shook her head. Even with her skin prickling and burning at the thought of radioactive particles clinging to her flesh, she couldn't bring herself to take off her tank top.

She'd hid her scars for so long. The thought of revealing them now, even here in the half-dark, sent chills zapping up her spine.

She was certain they'd made it in time to miss most of the fallout. She could afford to wait a few minutes for the bathroom to clear.

After she helped Zamira, Isabel, and Piper, she wrung out their clothes in the sinks as best she could, soapy water splashing all over the floor. They dressed in the cold, damp clothes, then rinsed out all the buckets.

Dakota, Shay, and Rasha refilled them to the brim with cold water and handed them to the women, who returned to auditorium seven, wet-haired, damp, and shivering, but clean.

Finally alone in the semi-darkness, Dakota shimmied out of her tank top, belt, and cargo pants. From the sheath attached to her belt, she pulled out the SOG Spec Arc tactical knife Ezra had given her on the only Christmas they'd spent at his cabin.

Unlike her XD9 or her bug out bag, it was one thing she could take with her everywhere—and she did. Ezra had taught her how to use it, too.

She swore she would never be helpless again, and she intended to keep that promise.

She set the knife carefully on the edge of the sink and went to work.

The air hit her exposed back like a slap. The skin around her scars prickled. She resisted the urge to shudder.

She cleaned herself quickly but thoroughly, scrubbing hard. A part of her wanted to rub her skin raw, just to ensure it was really clean, to make certain she'd gotten rid of every speck of contamination.

But of course, that was impossible.

The entire time, she managed not to look in the mirror, not even once.

14

LOGAN

Once everyone was finished, clothes wrinkled and wet but clean, they convened at the front of the auditorium.

Logan and Walter leaned against the wall near the pile of food and buckets of water, while Dakota and Rasha knelt next to the food, counting it all. Several people slumped in the plush seats, looking shell-shocked.

The teen boys sprawled beneath the theater screen, their dead phones limp in their hands. One sat with his knees tucked beneath his chin, narrow shoulders hunched. Wetness glimmered in the kid's dark eyes.

Gone was the punk posturing, the swagger; they were scared and homesick. They were soft, coddled by their mamas, weakened by summers immersed in air conditioning and video games.

At their age, Logan had already been on his own for nearly a year. Tough, defiant, recklessly aggressive. He'd won every fight, took on every challenger, accepted every problem and enemy as an opportunity to carve his own place in a brutal world.

And he had, piece by bloody piece.

Logan blinked and looked away sharply.

He didn't want to go where those thoughts led.

Instead, he watched as Shay went around with the first aid kit and tended to everyone's wounds with topical antibiotic gel and oversized butterfly Band-Aids.

Julio alone took up most of the medical supplies.

When Shay got to Logan, he waved the girl off.

The booth in the bar had spared him from most of the glass. The cuts on his arms from shielding his face weren't even bleeding anymore.

He picked out a last tiny shard from the jagged barb in the tattoo roping his left forearm.

He didn't look at the Latin phrase tangled within the barbs that wound around his arm. He never looked at it anymore if he could help it.

He glanced at the waitress and saw her watching him, a small, perplexed line forming between her brows.

A jolt of unease went through him, though he had no clue why.

He wanted to look away, but he forced himself to give her a lazy smile instead. Pretend he didn't give a damn hard enough, and eventually, it'd be true.

That's what he told himself, anyway.

"Do we have any idea how big this thing is?" Julio asked, absently rubbing the gold cross at his neck. "The blast, I mean."

Dakota broke eye contact. She sat back on her heels and shoved her chestnut hair behind her ears. "I'm going on the assumption that this bomb is an IND, an Improvised Nuclear Device, probably around ten kilotons. If it was a much larger nuke, we'd all be incinerated already."

"What does that mean?" Zamira asked.

She was listening intently from one of the theater seats, where she sat stroking her granddaughter's hair. The girl curled limply on her lap. Piper perched beside them, swinging her bare legs above the carpet.

"A kiloton measures the power of the explosion," Dakota explained. "The bomb that hit Nagasaki was ten kilotons. A thousand pounds of TNT equals one kiloton. So, imagine ten thousand pounds of TNT exploding at once, and you're starting to get the idea."

No one said anything for a long moment.

"It's the shockwave that devastates everything," Dakota said. "A blast three times as powerful as the worst category five hurricane."

Shay covered her mouth with her fingers and let out a gasp.

"And then there's the fallout," Dakota continued. "It's the most hazardous closest to ground zero. If you can see it—like what's outside—that stuff will give you a dose of radiation powerful enough to kill you within days or weeks.

"But just because you can't see it doesn't mean it still won't kill you, just maybe in weeks or months instead of days. And since you can't see it, you won't even know it's killing you until you get sick."

"If we get out of the immediate vicinity, will we be okay?" Zamira asked.

"No. The fallout follows the prevailing winds. Both the surface level we can feel, and the upper atmospheric winds we can't. It can spread and contaminate hundreds of square miles."

"We can't stay here for months!" cried a skinny, sunburned white guy in pleated khaki shorts and a salmon-pink golf shirt.

He'd introduced himself earlier as Miles. He seemed like the uptight, neurotic type, the kind who got hysterical over nothing instead of dealing with real problems head-on.

"We don't have to," Dakota said.

"We'll starve long before that!" Miles said.

"No, we won't," Logan said.

"We're trapped!" Miles screeched. "We can't survive in here—"

"Just shut up for a second, would you?" Dakota pressed her fingers against her temples, as if trying to block out the man's shrill whining.

Logan wanted to drown them out with a stiff drink, too. Or a punch to the vocal cords.

"Let's just take a breath," Julio said in a soothing voice. He played the peacemaker well, probably a skill he'd honed quelling hundreds of drunken fights as a bartender. "We should stay calm. Panic serves no purpose."

"I'm not panicking!" Miles said. "You're the one—"

"Just how long do we have to be in here?" the pretty, curvaceous Middle Eastern woman named Rasha asked, cutting the man off.

She stood next to Miles, her posture perfect, as she stroked his bright red forearm with her manicured fingers.

They were married, a head-scratcher of a pairing to Logan's mind—not because they were a mixed-race couple, but because Miles seemed like such a douchebag.

"My mom and sister live in Pinecrest," Rasha said evenly, with only a slight accent. "We were going to visit them tonight. We need to make sure they're okay."

"The fallout level decays fast, but—" Dakota started.

"How fast?" Miles interrupted. He shook off his wife's calming hand. "How many days?"

"It depends on the size of the blast and the wind and altitude—"

"Just tell us!" Miles snapped frantically.

"To be safe?" Dakota said, her voice measured and steady,

though a muscle twitched tensely at her jaw. "I think we need to remain here several days, maybe a week."

Logan's stomach sank. Seven days trapped in the dark and the heat with a handful of frantic, panicking strangers sounded like a special kind of torture.

Worse, his flask would run dry long before then. His mouth went dry at the thought.

Miles' eyes bulged. "A week? You've got to be kidding me. We're taking the first flight out of this hellhole!"

Logan couldn't disagree with the guy's assessment, even if he was a clueless schmuck. He shifted uneasily against the wall.

"What about our families? Our friends? My wife?" Julio asked. "We can't just leave them out there."

"You can't do anything for them now." The muscle in Dakota's jaw jumped. "What good will it do them if you go out there just to die? We have to wait. Then we can try to help them—"

"Enough is enough!" shouted a voice.

15

LOGAN

Logan watched as the heavy, thick-jowled woman with frizzed, coppery hair and furious eyes stormed down the far stairs from where she'd been sitting in the middle rows, a boy of about six trailing behind her.

He'd noticed her before when he'd conducted an initial scan of the auditorium. She hadn't come down to wash her clothes or help collect the water. She'd been sitting up there all this time, doing nothing but brooding.

The woman halted inches from Dakota, who'd risen to her feet at the first sign of trouble. She jabbed her finger at the waitress. "No one else seems capable of saying it, so I will. You're scaring my son to death with this nonsense!"

"What? No—" Dakota started.

"What are you? Some sort of doomsday cult? You all on drugs? This some sick joke you cooked up to prey on innocent, God-fearing citizens?"

Dakota raised her chin and didn't back down an inch. She batted the woman's finger away. "You better take a step back, lady."

Logan tensed. Instinctively, he stepped forward off the wall and uncrossed his arms, keeping his hands loose and ready at his sides. Just in case.

The woman dropped her finger but didn't lose an ounce of vitriol. Her gaze roamed over Logan's damp, wrinkled shirt and unkempt hair.

Her lip curled in derision. "I won't have it. My son has soccer practice. I have a dinner date. I have a life!"

She whirled on Schmidt. "You can bet I'll be demanding a refund and blowing up social media about this. This is the worst service I've ever experienced anywhere, in my life!"

"We saw it," Julio said, attempting diplomacy. "There was a blast, a flash of light—"

"Oh, a flash of light, was it?" the woman snarled. "Next thing you're gonna start spouting on about aliens."

The woman and her kid hadn't even left the auditorium after the blast. She hadn't left when the building trembled, the shockwave roared past, or when the power went out. She hadn't seen the windows shatter, the mushroom cloud, or the eerily darkening sky.

She'd simply sat there and waited, expecting the electricity to be restored and her movie—and her life—to continue on as normal.

"America is under attack," Zamira said solemnly. "At least three bombs have detonated—"

"No one's attacking America," the woman huffed. "No one would dare. Besides, even if they did, radiation is a myth. The danger is nothing like the scaremongers claim it is."

"I can assure you, the danger is very real," Dakota said through gritted teeth.

"Whatever this—" the woman waved her hand dismissively

"—event is, if it's even real, we're safest at home. That's where we're going."

"It's chaos out there." Dakota's voice went low and dangerous. "The fallout is still deadly. You're putting that boy in danger."

"No one's gonna tell me how to raise my family. That's it. We're outta here. You'll be hearing from my attorney for harassment, mark my words."

Dakota moved to stand in front of the woman, her hands balling into fists.

"Oh, you've got to be kidding me. I'm twice your size, girl. Whatever your game, I'm not playing. I'm going home."

Dakota didn't back down. "You go out there, you're gonna kill your kid, lady."

Logan wasn't a man for drama. He preferred a simple life with simple pleasures. When given a choice to get involved or walk away, he walked away ten times out of ten.

And yet—

The frightened gaze of the little boy peering around his mother's solid thigh wouldn't let him go. He felt the child's gaze like twin lasers boring into his soul.

Dakota could take care of herself. He could see it in her stance —feet shoulder-width apart, one leg slightly in front of the other for stability, balanced easily on the balls of her feet, hands loose at her sides. A good confrontational position, but one ready for defense—or offense.

Someone had taught her more than how to survive a nuclear apocalypse. She knew how to fight.

But even the best fighters needed a wingman, someone to have their back. The truth was, he didn't want that kid going out into the fallout any more than she did.

With a sigh, he strode across the aisle and stood beside Dakota. "Lady, it's real. Half the people here saw the mushroom cloud for themselves. You see the cuts all over Julio? He got those from the shockwave shattering every piece of glass within miles. Don't put your boy's life in danger. Wait even a day at least. Give yourself and him a fighting chance."

"You're the one scaring my kid," the woman snapped. "You can't keep us here. Let me pass."

He didn't move.

"You're scaring my kid, now. Is that what you wanted?" Her face purpled with anger—and fear. She seized her son's hand and yanked him against her side.

The boy looked up at him, blinking wide and frightened. His eyes were green, not dark brown. His fine, wispy hair was red like his mother's—not black and curly, like the hair that framed the face from his worst nightmares.

Logan jerked his gaze away. "No."

"They're trying to save your life, that's all," Julio said calmly from behind them.

"There's a few other kids here," Shay said. "You're welcome to stay—"

The woman ignored the others and kept her glare trained on Logan. "Then get the hell out of my way."

"This isn't right," Dakota said, her voice shaking.

"Dakota." Julio touched her arm, his voice soft and pleading. "I think it's best to let it be."

Julio was right. The woman wasn't going to stay unless they bodily restrained her. From the looks on everyone's faces, no one was ready to go to such an extreme.

Neither was he.

Logan pushed down a prick of guilt. This lady wasn't his problem. He had enough of his own right now. They all did.

He stepped aside and made a sweeping motion with his hand. "Suit yourself, lady."

Dakota stood there, trembling, her rigid expression betraying her anger.

But she didn't try to stop the woman as she stalked past them with a triumphant huff, dragging her son along behind her.

"Don't go home," Dakota called to her retreating back. "Travel as far as you can as fast as you can, and go perpendicular to the wind. It's your only chance."

The woman said nothing as she disappeared into the darkness, the clang of the doors echoing through the auditorium behind her.

16
LOGAN

For a long moment, everyone just stood there, staring at each other in shocked silence. Logan wished he were surprised, but he wasn't.

The world was full of the willfully ignorant. There wasn't a thing you could do about it. Getting all worked up over them was a waste of time and brain cells.

But that kid...those wide, haunted eyes wouldn't leave his mind.

"She knows which way to go," Shay said shakily. "Dakota warned her. Hopefully, they'll get out okay."

"No," Dakota said, her voice sharp as steel, her eyes flashing, "they won't."

"Forget her," Logan said. "They're beyond our help now, anyway. She made her choice. That's not on us."

Dakota shot him a look, but she didn't argue.

"You were explaining radiation," Julio said gently. "We still need to know this stuff. Keep going."

Dakota sucked in a sharp breath. She turned away from the

auditorium doors and faced the group. Her hands were still balled into fists at her sides.

"How will we know when it's safe to go outside?" Julio prompted.

"Okay," Dakota said. "So, radioactive fallout decays exponentially. The highest hazard from fallout is within the first four to six hours. I believe the worst of it will descend to the ground within twenty-four hours."

"You *believe*?" Schmidt scoffed. "How are we supposed to trust you with our lives? You could be making this up, for all we know!"

"She's right," Shay offered. "I'm a third-year nursing student at the U. I'm also a registered volunteer first responder. I took a disaster preparedness and response seminar last January. We covered medical responses to nuclear disasters as part of the certification. Risk assessment, decontamination procedures, triage and emergency patient care in the field, et cetera."

Dakota dipped her chin to acknowledge Shay's support. "Look, I'm no expert. But someone extremely smart—and well-prepared—taught me what he knew. That knowledge is gonna keep us alive."

"Bah!" Schmidt sputtered. "You're both barely out of high school! Just two more millennial morons who think they know everything—"

"Just let them talk," Logan cut in. What little patience he had was already long gone. "Then you can decide what you want to believe."

Several people nodded in agreement. Miles folded his arms across his chest. Schmidt shot Logan a look of pure loathing, but he kept his mouth shut.

He didn't care whether the asshat hated him. He didn't care whether they all hated him.

"It's called the seven-ten rule," Dakota said. "For every sevenfold *increase* in time after the detonation, there's a ten-fold *decrease* in the exposure rate. Or, when the amount of time is multiplied by seven, the exposure rate is divided by ten.

"In a nutshell, in twenty-four hours, the radiation dose will be at ten percent of what it is now. In forty-eight hours, it will be at one percent."

"So then we can get out of here and find my mom," Piper chirped. She looked as earnestly hopeful as a lost puppy. "Right?"

Dakota shook her head. "It's still far from safe. I estimate we're about a mile and a half from the blast, but we're downwind, directly in the path of the fallout, which could be as high as one thousand rem an hour right now—"

"What does that mean?" Logan asked. "I flunked high school chemistry." In reality, he'd dropped out of high school at sixteen, but no one needed to know that.

"A Roentgen is a way to measure the amount of radiation emitted at the moment," Dakota said. "Rem means 'Roentgen Equivalent Man.' Rem measures the amount of radiation that's present, while the unit of measurement for the dose a person absorbs is called a gray.

"Just remember that rem refers to the amount of radiation in an area, while gray refers to the dose absorbed by a person. 100 rem is equal to one gray. And the exposure is cumulative."

"And what do the dosages mean?" Julio asked, his brow wrinkling in confusion.

"I know this one," Shay said. "Between one and two grays the typical person succumbs to acute radiation syndrome, with nausea and vomiting, headaches, and lethargy. Many people can survive lower doses of radiation, but at higher levels, it will kill them."

"How many people are already dead?" Zamira's wobbly chin lifted bravely as she stroked her granddaughter's hair, but tears glistened in her dark eyes. Piper nestled next to her, her head on the old woman's shoulder, her glasses still crooked on her nose.

"We don't know," Julio said. "Tens of thousands. Maybe more."

"There were three bombs?" Rasha asked.

"That we know of," Julio said in a strained voice.

Several people wiped away tears. Others stared in numb shock, unable to grasp the magnitude of the atrocity that had overtaken them.

Logan's mind kept shying away from it, trying to brush the heinous numbers aside, to pretend it couldn't possibly be this horrific. He forced himself to accept it, to adjust to this new reality as quickly as he could.

"Tens of thousands of people near ground zero will be exposed to fatal doses of radiation," Dakota said. "Hundreds of thousands more will have to evacuate from their homes due to the fallout. But even after everyone is evacuated, the area will be contaminated."

Logan found himself leaning forward despite himself. He might have been a dropout, but he'd always had a keen mind for acquiring valuable information.

Rasha gasped in dismay.

"Rain will wash away contaminated soil within a few weeks or months," Dakota said, "but urban and suburban areas are a different story. Homes, schools, hospitals, prisons, and factories will be unusable. The government will have to demolish buildings and undertake extensive decontamination measures."

"That will take years," Logan said.

For a moment, they all stared at each other, letting the overwhelming horror sink in. The destruction would be enormous, with far-reaching consequences they couldn't even imagine yet.

"Mother Mary and Joseph," Julio murmured, crossing himself. "God help us all."

Zamira fingered a cluster of prayer beads she'd pulled from her pocket. "We should pray for all the lost and suffering souls."

Prayer had never done anything for Logan. Only one thing worked, though never for long.

That burning urge filled him, a *wanting* always clawing at his insides, a hissing whisper haunting his every thought.

What he wouldn't give for a bottle of Absolut vodka or Jack Daniel's whiskey. Why couldn't they have found refuge in one of those dine-in, full wine-list cinemas?

Now that would be a fine way to ride out the apocalypse.

17

EDEN

Eden pressed her fist to her mouth in terror. She gasped in frantic, silent sobs, her body quaking with tremor after tremor, like the aftershocks of an earthquake.

But this was no earthquake.

The roaring noise had stopped. The shaking had stopped. The light blaring through the cracks in the door frame had faded.

There was only the darkness now. Black so thick and soupy she couldn't make out her hands in front of her face.

She strained her ears, listening for people, for her foster parent, for someone coming to rescue her. The only sound was the *drip, drip, drip* of the water in the sink. And the thump of her own heartbeat in her ears.

The bathroom smelled like the lemon cleaner the maid used. Her spine dug into the bottom of the hard porcelain tub. Her shoulders and neck ached. Her knees were bent awkwardly, her bare feet pushed against the far tub wall beneath the faucet.

The oversized sofa cushion she'd pulled on top of her was scratchy, one of the zippers digging into her neck. Beneath it, she clutched the notepad to her chest, her fingers like claws.

But she didn't dare move.

She knew what the bright flash was, what it meant.

A nuclear bomb.

Was this the judgment her father preached about? Armageddon plunging down from the heavens in a raging onslaught of boiling smoke and fire?

Dakota had warned her.

So had Ezra, all those years ago, when he'd let them stay in his cabin on the edge of the swamp. It had seemed so far from civilization, it might as well have been located at the edge of the world.

That was how she felt now—like she'd slipped off the edge of the planet and was lost somewhere in another dimension, or maybe a black hole.

She didn't know how bad it was. She didn't know anything.

Outside her tiny, claustrophobic bathroom, the whole world could be destroyed. The entire house could be buried beneath a ton of rubble so deep no one would ever be able to dig her out, even if they could hear her screams.

Which they couldn't. Because she had no voice. No way to reach out to anyone beyond these four cramped walls. She was stuck in here in the darkness, with only the tub, the sink and toilet, the chilly tile floor.

All she knew was that she couldn't leave until someone came for her. If they came for her. *Dakota promised.*

She was all alone. All alone in the darkness she feared, the darkness where the monsters could creep in, both imaginary and real.

She moaned, her throat making a rough, ruined sound. Tears leaked down her cheeks, snot bubbling in her nose.

She wanted her foster parents.

She missed them. She missed them with a hollow ache in the

center of her chest, almost as much as she missed Dakota, her father, and her brothers.

She wanted Gabriella's warm, comforting presence sitting next to her as she fell back into a bruised, restless sleep, brushing her damp hair back from her face and humming some Spanish pop song Eden didn't know the words to.

She wanted Jorge to bring her another one of his favorite books—*1984* or *Animal Farm*—and read to her long into the night, even when he had to get up early for work the next day.

In those first weeks at the Rosses without Dakota, the nightmares had stalked her every night.

She couldn't cry out after a nightmare. She had no way to alert them to her distress, her terror.

She'd thrashed in her bed in the dark, choking on her own whispery, rasping moans, silent sobs shaking her whole body, too frightened to leave her room.

Only when she'd fallen out of bed one night did they glimpse her night terrors. Instinctively, she'd cowered against the wall, scrambling for her notepad to babble an explanation, to frantically apologize and promise to never wake them again.

They hadn't responded like her real father used to, with belittling anger and shame. The next day, Jorge rigged an alarm button on her nightstand. When she pushed it, his phone buzzed, alerting them.

The Rosses always came together, both of them.

Eden liked them. Loved them even, though she didn't dare tell Dakota that.

Gabriella was a kind-hearted poet; Jorge, a pediatrician with a wicked sense of humor.

It was Gabriella who gave her the gift of language, signing her up for American Sign Language classes, who bought her artist-quality pencils and drawing supplies.

Jorge opened up a world of books and reading—books that would've been banned in her old life at the compound. But Jorge let her read anything she wanted to.

She dreaded telling Dakota the truth—she wanted the Rosses to adopt her. Even though she loved Dakota with every beat of her heart. Even though she knew Dakota desperately wanted to be named her legal guardian.

She longed to be part of a real family again.

She felt torn between her affection for the Rosses and her loyalty to Dakota. Fear and guilt and loss snarled inside her.

Maybe it didn't even matter. Maybe her foster parents were already dead. Maybe Dakota was, too. Maybe every single person in the whole state of Florida was already dead.

Her mind shied away from that thought.

No. Gabriella and Jorge were still out there, trying to find their way home. And Dakota was coming for her, too.

Slowly, her sobs subsided. She dried her salty tears with the back of her arm. Her hitched breaths slowed.

She clutched her notebook to her chest and stared up into the thick, looming blackness, imagining the shape of the ceiling above her.

Dakota was the toughest person she knew. She never gave up.

Eden loved her foster parents, but it was Dakota she put her faith in.

18

LOGAN

"You got people out there?" Julio asked Logan quietly.

They were slumped against the wall, staring out at the silent, darkened theater. The few flashlight beams cast everything in an eerie, ghostly glow. Time was passing, but Logan didn't know how much. It couldn't go fast enough.

But when he finally got out of here, where would he even go?

Logan had no girlfriend at home, no dog waiting eagerly, tail waving. No friends, really. Whatever family he'd had once had disowned him long ago.

He went to work, he went to the gym and the bar, he came home to a nondescript apartment, empty of anything but the bare essentials—a mattress, a fridge full of beer, and a cabinet lined with wine and booze.

The next day, he did it all again. It was a small, careful, barren life.

But it was the life he deserved, wasn't it?

Now, just when he thought he was getting his equilibrium back, he was knocked on his ass again. Big time.

"Nah," he said. "There's no one to miss me."

"My wife's in West Palm Beach visiting her sister." Julio's voice was shaky. His left knee was juddering like crazy. "Never had kids. Never could, you know? I'm thinking now, maybe that was a blessing.

"My wife's sister though, she's got two little Cuban hellions. Five and seven. One's into princesses and ponies; the other one's always got dirt beneath her nails, bests every boy in her class at soccer and softball. Don't know what I'd do if we lost those girls..."

In the bar, it was always Julio who soothed everyone else, always offering a listening ear, a comforting shoulder to cry on. Logan didn't know what to say. That it was better to have no one, to only need to worry about yourself?

It was the only way he'd survived. Don't give an enemy a single point of vulnerability. No one and nothing could hurt him.

But he couldn't say that to Julio, whose face was drawn from worry over his family. At the bar, all Logan had to do was drink until he was good and boozy and then drink some more. He left the serious talk to Julio and the others.

He wanted a drink right now. He slipped his silver flask out of his pocket, unscrewed the lid, and allowed himself one long, sweet swallow.

He'd have to make it last, but damn if he didn't want to down the whole thing now.

"I'm sorry, man," he said. The silence between them had suddenly deepened like a pit he'd fall into if he didn't say something, no matter how lame.

"I'm no hero." Julio gazed forlornly down at his phone. "I'm scared to death, to be perfectly honest. But I can't just leave her out there. She's—she needs me. What kind of man would I be if I didn't go after her?"

"One that's still alive."

Julio gave a pained snort. "I feel so guilty. Every second that passes…it just gets worse."

It always surprised him how easily and openly Julio discussed his feelings. Like it was perfectly normal, like guilt wasn't a heavy, clanking chain choking his throat, wasn't a ruinous cancer slowly poisoning him from the inside out.

Logan's guilt was a dark, toxic murk he buried deep and thought of as little as possible.

He opened his mouth, though he had not a clue what to say.

"What about iodine?" Rasha asked from a few yards away. Her question offered a blessed respite from the strained conversation. Logan shifted slightly, giving the woman his full attention.

Rasha perched on the edge of her seat, her ankles crossed, absently tapping the useless phone she still held with her fingernails, as if it might magically power up.

She frowned as she adjusted her hijab. "I read this apocalyptic novel once where China nuked us, and everyone was rushing to take iodine to protect against the radiation. Do we need to worry about that?"

"I'll take that one," Shay said, sitting cross-legged against the far wall. "It's kind of a myth that it's some lifesaving medicine, actually. A nuclear bomb or power plant meltdown releases radioactive iodine into the air, which people then inhale. It's absorbed by the thyroid and could potentially cause cancer.

"Ideally, if you take potassium iodide, or KI, right before or right after exposure, it blocks the radioactive iodine from the nuclear blast from entering your thyroid. If the thyroid absorbs all the iodine that it needs from the nonradioactive KI, then the radioactive iodine won't be absorbed, and gets eliminated through urine."

"Eww," Piper squeaked.

Shay popped her gum. "Exactly."

"So, it doesn't cause cancer?" Zamira asked.

"If radioactive iodine does build up in your thyroid, it could cause cancer, yeah. But people over forty have almost no risk of developing thyroid cancer from radioiodine. They're more likely to suffer side effects from taking the KI, though, like rashes, nausea, and allergic reactions. Kids, too.

"Besides, even if you took it in time and kept your body from absorbing it, radioiodine is just a tiny fraction of the overall radiation exposure. The iodine doesn't protect your body from any of the other 99% of radioactive nuclides." Shay hesitated. "You're much better off concerning yourself with finding an adequate shelter. Otherwise, you're rearranging deck chairs on the Titanic."

Rasha nodded, her shoulders sagging slightly, and stared down at the phone clenched in her manicured hands. "I feel like that's what we're doing anyway. Rearranging furniture on a sinking ship."

Logan grunted. "It'd be a faster death."

Dakota shot him a hard look.

He shrugged. It was the truth, wasn't it? All this depressing talk just made him want to bury his head in a bottle.

"We're fine," Shay said brightly, her voice too loud and chipper in the somber auditorium. She popped her gum as she grinned appreciatively back at Logan and Julio, then Dakota. "We're gonna be okay. You guys saved us."

"It was Dakota," Julio said. "She did it."

Shay beamed at Dakota. "Thank you."

The waitress shifted uncomfortably. She cleared her throat, like she wasn't used to the praise and didn't care for it. "I did what I had to. Anyone else would do the same."

Somehow Logan doubted that.

He would have left them all.

19
DAKOTA

"Hey," Julio said quietly as he came up beside Dakota. She sat in the first row of seats with her knees drawn up to her chest, staring dully at the big white screen as if it could give her the answers she desperately needed.

It hadn't given her anything.

She kept replaying the scene with the woman and her son over and over in her head, trying to change the scenario so the woman stayed.

It didn't work.

Just the thought of that woman's smug, arrogant face filled Dakota with fury. It wasn't right. It was a parent's job to protect their child, no matter what.

Dakota had never understood those kinds of people, the ones who'd put a child in danger for their own selfish, irrational desires.

Some of her foster parents had been like that—only in it for the money, their cruelty driven by indifference, greed, or willful ignorance.

And Maddox, Solomon, and their ilk—they were a whole different breed of cruel.

Acid burned the back of her throat. She swallowed it down. Those were the bad memories, the ones she didn't think about anymore.

She couldn't bear to think about what was happening to that little boy outside, the toxic radiation invading his skin, his cells, his bones.

The same thing was happening to tens of thousands of people who hadn't found shelter, who hadn't known what to do.

So many people without the knowledge to react quickly, to save their lives and the lives of the ones they loved.

And then there were those given the facts, who still chose to ignore the reality right in front of them. They just didn't want to face it. They were cowards at heart, cowards and fools who endangered the lives of everyone around them.

She clenched her teeth, her hands balled into fists. She needed to calm down, to focus. *One. Two. Three. Breathe.*

"Hello? Earth to Dakota."

She glanced up at Julio. "Yeah?"

He sank into the empty seat beside her with a groan. "You okay?"

He looked older than he had just that morning. Shadows bruised the skin below his eyes, and deep lines bracketed his mouth. His hair seemed grayer, his face strained. Two dozen large Band-Aids peppered his arms, neck, and left cheek.

She hated seeing Julio like this. He was a decent guy, easygoing and good-natured. Kind when he didn't have to be.

She had no patience for most people, but she liked him.

"I should ask you that," she said. "You feeling okay?"

"Don't worry about me." He gave a tight smile and lowered his voice. "Tell me the truth. How bad is it really? How protected are we in here?"

She sighed. "Protection levels vary based on building type,

construction, location within the building, even time from detonation. It's impossible to say for sure."

"You're a smart girl, and you know your stuff. What's your best guess?"

She leaned her head back against the seat and squinted until the white screen blurred. "Well, there are three main types of radiation. Alpha particles can't penetrate human skin. They can only hurt you if you inhale or swallow them.

"Beta radiation can't penetrate a sheet of aluminum foil, but it can cause bad burns if the particles come in contact with bare skin. Regular clothes provide a good barrier.

"But gamma radiation is the most dangerous threat. Gamma rays penetrate almost everything. Think of each gamma particle as an LED light shining brilliantly in all directions. Now multiply that by millions. Any light that reaches you is radiation.

"We need to shield ourselves from all that light, and from all directions—from the ground, the sides, and the roof. Mass is what matters; the denser the material, the better."

She closed her eyes, recalling the faded charts old Ezra had told her to memorize. "Shielding is measured by the fraction of gamma rays that it blocks. If a certain thickness—say two inches of concrete—blocks half of the incoming radiation, it has a protection factor, or PF, of 2. A PF of 10 means you'd receive one-tenth the dose inside versus outside."

"Like the SPF of sunscreen."

"Exactly."

Julio groaned. "I can't believe you're making me do math. Math and the apocalypse do not go together."

She shrugged. Math had never been difficult for her.

"What do you think we have? We're on the ground floor, but there's a floor above us. At least five decent-sized stores on either side of us. The whole complex is heavy construction."

"The FEMA minimum-required PF in public shelters is 40, I think. I hope this is at least 40 PF, but I don't know for sure."

She squinted at the huge blank screen above them. What had Ezra always said? *When you need to know this, it'll already be too late.*

"And a regular house?"

"A wood-frame house only has a PF of 4 at most. Not enough."

She thought of Eden, who hadn't had time to shelter anywhere better than a two-story house. At least it was a big one.

Would it be enough? She could only hope the fallout cloud stayed to the east and Eden escaped the worst of it. It was her sister's only chance.

"Mainly, you want to take shelter underground. If you can't, then the middle, inner rooms of a large building away from doors and windows will work. A house sucks, but it's better than nothing."

Julio gestured toward the hallway leading to the auditorium doors. "And out there? How bad is the radiation?"

She closed her eyes and sighed heavily. "That's the question, isn't it? Without a Geiger counter, I have no idea. All I know is, it's high. I wish I could tell you more."

"You did great." Julio patted her arm. "You saved us. You're a hero."

Dakota shook her head, heat creeping up her throat. It was Ezra who'd given her the knowledge to survive. She hadn't done anything special to deserve it.

And she hadn't done anything heroic to save these people. She hadn't even been able to save that kid from the idiocy of his mother.

In the end, she was just as helpless as everyone else.

20

DAKOTA

An hour or so later, Shay came up to Dakota and Julio as she popped a stick of gum in her mouth. She offered it to them; they shook their heads.

She stuffed the package in her back pocket. "Sorry to bother you guys, but what do you think about the food? Travis's already complaining of hunger. He's a stick, but he'll eat a fridge-worth of food. Maybe we should divvy it up?"

"Good thinking," Zamira said. "If we're here for at least a week, then we need to make sure we have enough food to last."

Zamira hadn't fallen apart like some of the others. She seemed like a practical, no-nonsense *abuela,* almost like Sister Rosemarie from the compound.

Dakota's chest tightened. A flood of memories threatened to cascade over her. She shoved them out of her head. There was no time for self-pity in the apocalypse.

"We should come up with a rationing plan," she said instead.

Zamira gave her granddaughter a playful nudge, trying to get some life out of the girl. "No hogging, *sí?*"

The girl didn't respond, though Piper smiled wanly.

Dakota forced herself to nod. She suddenly felt incredibly tired. "We have fifteen people and four hundred and forty-seven total items of packaged chips, candies, and cookies. To last seven days, we can only give out four packages per person a day."

"That's not enough!" cried Travis, the scrawny, redheaded assistant manager. "I'll starve!"

Rasha gestured at the food pile with pursed lips. "How do we know this food is even safe to eat? We could be poisoning ourselves with every bite."

Dakota surveyed the food. "It's impossible for it to be irradiated. Radiation is only released the instant of detonation. After that, nothing becomes radioactive. The fallout is from the initial event—no new radiation is created.

"If fallout particles fall into opened food or water through broken pipes, then it might become contaminated. If you eat or drink it, radioactive particles will get inside your body. But anything sealed at the time of detonation is safe."

Rasha and Travis just stared at her blankly.

"Here—pretend cockroaches are scurrying around everywhere, touching everything, but anything the cockroach can't get to is safe—the bottled water is fine because the cockroach can't get inside it."

"That makes sense," Shay said helpfully.

Schmidt swaggered over with a scornful scowl. "It's my food. I'm keeping a close watch on everything." He brandished a pen and notepad at them. "And I'll be keeping track of what everyone owes, mark my words!"

Dakota clenched her teeth. This guy was getting on her last nerve. "I'll be happy to pay for it. Just as soon as the banks open tomorrow."

To keep herself as anonymous and unfindable as possible, she didn't use a bank or credit cards, but he didn't know that.

Besides, she had a feeling the banks wouldn't be opening for a while.

She was half-tempted to open the back hatch of her phone case and slide out the neatly folded emergency cash she always kept on hand—two hundred dollars—just to shut him up.

She tried not to think of her savings stashed in a hole in the wall she'd covered with one of Eden's paintings. Right now, it was as good as gone.

If her abysmal apartment was damaged, it might be literally gone, simply burned into ash. And she'd already lost her bug out bag. So many supplies she'd carefully researched and purchased over the last two years, all the preparations she'd made.

Gone in an instant.

All she had left was the two hundred dollars.

Who knew when banks and ATMs and credit cards would work again? When would the power return? A few days? A few months?

What if there were more than three bombs? What would happen to the country then?

She pushed that thought out of her head and focused on the now. Once she got Eden, they would need food, shelter, and fresh supplies for their journey.

Cash was critical.

"Here." Julio dug his wallet out of his back pocket and offered Schmidt a credit card and a wrinkled twenty-dollar bill. "However much the food costs, you can charge my card in full as soon as this is all over."

"Julio—" Dakota started, frustration flaring through her. Her boss was too kindhearted for his own good. Schmidt was the jerk-face. Schmidt was the one who needed a good slap across his fat, greedy face—

"Fine by me." Schmidt seized Julio's credit card, stuck it in the breast pocket of his manager's uniform, and returned to pacing in front of the stockpile of supplies like a king protecting his castle from infidels.

Dakota jumped to her feet and strode up the steps toward the rear seats, as far away from people as she could get before she threw a punch at someone.

She hadn't even been stuck in here a full day and she was already claustrophobic, anxious, and irritated as hell. It would be a miracle if she managed to stay sane for the next forty-eight hours, let alone a week.

She sank into one of the seats in the back corner and allowed herself to ease her head against the cushioned headrest. She shivered, her clothes still slightly damp. At least she was alone.

Still, she didn't close her eyes. She needed to sleep, to rest and gather her strength for the arduous journey ahead—but she didn't trust these people as far as she could throw them.

The thought of letting her guard down made her chest tighten, her gut twisting with apprehension.

She knew better than anyone that danger could come from any quarter, especially from scared and desperate people.

Her muscles were tensed and knotted, her stomach a cement brick. More than anything, she hated this sense of overwhelming helplessness.

Eden was out there—trapped, maybe hurt, certainly terrified. Had she been exposed to radiation? Was she slowly dying right now?

And there was Maddox, still a lethal presence stalking the edges of Dakota's consciousness, a shadow she couldn't escape from.

If he'd survived the blast, he wouldn't let a bomb stop him from hunting down his prey and taking his prize. He was the most single-minded, determined person she'd ever met.

No, he wasn't dead. She wasn't lucky enough.

He was still out there, hunting. Coming for Eden, defenseless and unprotected.

Dakota longed to *do* something, to get the hell out of here and save her sister, but she couldn't, not yet. She couldn't do anything. She wouldn't do anyone a lick of good by exposing herself to deadly levels of radiation and dying within a week.

No matter what, she had to keep her head.

Eden needed her.

21
MADDOX

Maddox moaned. His mouth felt gritty and metallic, like it was full of dirt and copper. Sounds came to him slowly, tinny and distant.

He didn't know how much time passed. His ears were ringing. White spots floated in front of his eyes. Blood dripped from somewhere.

Slowly, gingerly, he found he could move his hands, his arms, then his legs. Pain spiked through him, but he ignored it. He unsnapped his seatbelt and fumbled for the door handle.

It wouldn't budge. The door wasn't in the right shape anymore. Dimly, he became aware that the taxi had crumpled around him like a soda can.

The taxi driver hung limply, his head bloodied and lolling at a disturbing, unnatural angle, his body still bound in place by his seatbelt. The steering wheel had crushed his sternum. He was no longer alive.

The right-side rear door looked untouched. He stretched across the back seat, every part of his body aching, sharp stabs of agony flaring through his shoulder, and wrestled the door open. Wincing, he eased himself from the taxi.

He collapsed to the concrete and pulled himself up with a groan. He was still in the tunnel. Emergency lights flickered red, bathing the tunnel walls in an eerie glow. It was dim, but he could see clearly enough.

The cars were no longer in straight, orderly lines. Some had toppled to their sides, wheels still spinning; others were upside down, their roofs caved-in, metal skeletons smashed, crushed, and broken.

Up and down the tunnel, every car and truck and SUV was a wreck of twisted, smoking metal. Several cars had caught fire. It was like a giant had seized the vehicles and hurled them at the walls and ceiling, at each other.

But that didn't make sense. His brain was fuzzy, his thoughts coming scattered and disjointed. He must have suffered a concussion from the crash.

He was alone in the tunnel. Several car doors hung open; those who'd survived had abandoned their ruined cars and fled. Car alarms blared, echoing off the tunnel walls.

How long had he blacked out? Minutes? Hours?

It felt like a long time. It felt like a whole lifetime had passed in the blink of an eye.

He checked his phone, but it was dead. He felt for his holster—the Beretta was still there.

He turned, searching for the closest tunnel entrance, only a few hundred yards back the way he'd come.

He blinked and looked again.

At the end of the tunnel, the sun was gone.

Part of the tunnel had collapsed.

Mountains of rubble blocked the tunnel entrance: chunks of pipe and concrete, cables twisting like pythons, bits of metal and plastic, and a great slab of concrete tumbled from the ceiling jaunting at nearly a ninety-degree angle.

A triangle of yellow haze shone through.

A gap existed. A gap he could escape through.

He staggered toward the strange, dim light. Gagging on the choking dust, he ignored the pain groaning through his body and groped through the rubble, pushing and pulling twisted beams and chunks of collapsed wall and ceiling aside.

And then, finally, he was out.

Maddox exited the tunnel. A jumble of burning, wrecked cars blocked the entire causeway ahead of him.

He stood, stunned and gaping, taking in the ruins before him.

The sun was setting, but he could barely tell.

A massive, boiling cloud loomed over Miami.

Everything below the cloud was burning. Thick black smoke roiled up from hundreds of fires. Everywhere seethed dust and smoke and fire.

The skyline was wrong.

Skyscrapers that had reached for the sky before were gone.

The tops of forty-story buildings were simply sheared off. Some were gouged, as if a gigantic monster had gorged itself on steel.

Still others were blackened steel skeletons, warped and bent, jutting into the sky like broken teeth.

It looked like the end of the world, as though the Armageddon he'd always heard about had descended with a violent, shuddering fury, to punish the whole Earth.

The sight filled him with a terrible awe.

It was both beautiful and terrifying.

22

DAKOTA

The hours inched by with agonizing slowness. Dakota's eyes burned with exhaustion, but she refused to sleep. Anxiety tangled in her gut. She kept thinking of Ezra and the cabin—the only place she'd ever felt safe.

Dakota tilted the flashlight inside the plastic cupholder on the arm of the seat and fumbled in the side pocket of her black cargo pants, feeling the comforting security of the knife against her hip.

She pulled out the folded sheet of paper she'd always kept with her.

The knife. The drawing. The bug out bag. Those were the three things she'd kept on her person as much as physically possible.

She smoothed the paper—thinning now, and a bit ragged at the folds after two years of use. It was one of Eden's drawings, excellently rendered as usual.

The cabin in the woods, Eden called it. But it wasn't just a cabin; it was a small fortress. And it wasn't in the woods; it was in the Everglades.

In the drawing, a simple wood-slat cabin with a flat tin roof squatted about two-thirds up the page, surrounded by hulking cypress trees, with white mangroves standing along the edges.

The lower half of the drawing featured a swamp spiked with saw grass, and a two-seater air-boat nestled among the stalks, almost hidden.

The address of Eden's foster family was also hidden, carefully embedded vertically in the bark of one of the cypress trees along the left-hand side of the page.

Dakota had memorized the address long ago, but she still kept the drawing.

That innocuous-looking house nestled in the middle of a swamp was her home in a way nothing had been since her parents died nine years ago, when she was ten. She hadn't said goodbye when she'd been forced to flee with Eden two years ago. She hoped they'd be welcomed back now.

This cabin was their destination. It was the only place she knew that offered safety, security, and three years' worth of prepped food and supplies.

No matter what chaos was coming—and she had an uneasy feeling that Ezra would be proven right, again—that place was a bunker in any storm.

Her mind dragged her back to the day she and Eden had first stumbled upon it, both of them dirty, bleeding, hungry, and terrified.

Three years ago, Dakota had been sixteen; Eden, only twelve.

It was a midsummer night deep in the Everglades. Cicadas serenaded each other in the hot, still air. Mosquitoes whined in her ears. Humidity clung to her skin, sweat beading her forehead, her neck, under her arms.

But she'd barely felt any of that.

They were fleeing the River Grass Compound—fleeing what Dakota had done, what waited for Eden.

Blood stained Dakota's trembling hands, her face. But it wasn't hers.

Some of it was Eden's.

Her heart galloping in her chest, her breath choking her throat, and the burn searing her back like acid, she grasped Eden's hand and ran.

Their long skirts flapping around their legs, they ran past the small shacks, winding around the garden and storage sheds to the guard platform that should've been manned but wasn't, and down through the trees to the edge of the swamp.

She knew where they kept the airboats, the keys hidden within the picture frame hanging on the wall of the boathouse. She even knew how to operate one.

Maddox and his brother Jacob had taken her out in secret a dozen times. Back before they'd become the enemy.

But she couldn't think about that.

Wincing as the burned skin on her back stretched, she grabbed the keys and a flashlight hanging from a steel hook. Her blood-stained hands left a smear of red behind.

They would know she'd been here. Hopefully by then, they'd already be gone.

She paused at the edge of the muddy bank, staring at the miles and miles of saw grass puncturing a sea of still, dark water. Clumps of trees sprouted from the river of grass here and there.

Everything was the same, as far as the eye could see, stretching into the darkness. Fear throbbed through every cell in her body. The Glades was wild and dangerous. There were a hundred different ways to die.

It was the only place they could get lost.

And if they were lost, then they couldn't be found.

There was one road out of the compound. Had they tried to

take that, the Shepherds would've tracked them down within an hour.

This way, at least they had a chance.

What lay behind them was worse than what lay before them. She had to believe that.

Beside her, Eden let out a faint moan.

Forcing herself to move, she clenched her jaw as the welt just above her shoulder blade pulsed with heat, searing fresh and raw with her every movement.

One, two, three. Breathe.

Endure the pain. That was all she could do. If they didn't get out of there, another burn would be the least of her problems.

Dakota sat gingerly on the seat mounted in front of the cage that housed the propeller. The boat was aluminum, about twelve feet long, and narrow.

The engine was mounted on metal scaffolding a few feet in front of the stern. A seat was bolted to a square platform lifted several feet in the air, with the passenger seat anchored below it.

Dakota pulled a small waterproof bag from beneath the passenger seat, dug around inside it, and handed her sister earplugs. She twisted hers in, too.

She put the key in the ignition, pumped the rubber-button choke three times, and turned the key. The engine belched smoke and roared to life, the propellers spinning, shaking the boat.

Eden grabbed the edges of her seat. Her eyes were glassy and unfocused, blood still dribbling from the gash in her throat, despite the torn shirt Dakota had wrapped around her neck.

"Hold on tight," she shouted, though her sister didn't seem to hear her over the engine.

If Eden lost her grip and fell in the water...she could swim, but could she swim injured? Would her blood attract the bull gators, like sharks in a feeding frenzy?

Dakota gritted her teeth and fought off the panic. There was enough to worry about already. She had to have faith that her sister could do this, that they could do this.

She eased the throttle forward, adding gas slowly until they were skimming along the water at a good pace, using the steering stick to turn, pushing the stick right to go left, left to go right.

She glanced at the small GPS screen that told her where she needed to go—twenty-five miles to the levee.

She didn't know where after that. A cheap hotel in Everglades City, maybe. Just away, somewhere far from here, somewhere safe.

They skimmed across the surface of the water. She could barely hear her own panicked, whirring thoughts over the engine. Her bare arms and legs stung from the flecks of saw grass flying at them—the airboat was like a lawnmower.

She wiped off dots of blood and ignored the pain.

What they needed were pants, boots, and long-sleeved shirts to protect against the sharp-edged saw grass. But they were both dressed in long skirts and short-sleeved blouses, the restrictive garb Dakota had been forced to wear since the first day she arrived at the compound.

After her parents died in a car accident, her devout, dour Aunt Ida had agreed to take her in, shipping her across the country to the commune where she lived and worked—the River Grass Compound, home of the Shepherds of Mercy.

But that was a lifetime ago.

The minutes passed achingly slow. She kept twisting around in her seat, half-expecting the lights from a pursuing airboat to pin her in their harsh glare.

But there was nothing.

The moonlight silvered everything. The tree islands floated like dark ships on a glowing sea. She motored past the hammocks and straight through the clumps of saw grass and cattails.

Using the nav lights, she kept her eyes peeled for water moccasins—not that she'd see them in the dark—and gators. There were always gators.

Everything was deadly here.

A dozen small pairs of red orbs peered at her just above the surface of the brackish water—alligator eyes. With the tapetum lucidum at the back of each eye reflecting light back into their photoreceptor cells, gator eyes reflected a red, devilish glow.

It felt like Satan's minions were watching them, just waiting for their chance to pounce.

Eden hunched in her seat, shivering, though it was far from cold. She needed a doctor, but Dakota couldn't give that to her.

"Only a little while more," she said, but Eden didn't respond.

They passed a strip of dry land covered with a few low bushes and several hammocks—islands made of trees, walls of cattails, and dense stands of saw grass. She aimed toward a narrow channel, passing through a thick stand of cattails on either side.

The engine sputtered. The airboat rocked and slowed. Dakota checked the gas, a sickening sensation churning in her belly.

In her frantic bid to escape, she hadn't checked. She'd picked an airboat with less than a quarter tank of gas.

They weren't anywhere near the levee yet.

Damn. Damn. Damn. What now?

She scanned the endless water, the grass, the trees, panic clawing up her throat.

There. About thirty yards ahead to the right. An old, rotting dock leading to a peninsula of dry land thick with cypress and mangrove trees.

Jutting from the water along the muddy bank, a weathered wooden sign splattered the words in red, dripping paint: TRESSPASSERS WILL BE SHOT.

On one of their trips, Maddox had taken her past this same

dock, pointing it out, shouting gleefully, "That's crazy old Ezra's place. Don't get too close, or the ole codger'll shoot your head off. For real."

Did she have a choice now? The airboat was nearly out of gas. Without the boat's GPS, she couldn't tell which way to go.

They were too far from the levee, from a road, from any speck of civilization.

Without the boat, they'd need to walk and swim through miles of swamp, through gator-infested waters, through a directionless wasteland of saw grass and cattails that went on and on and on.

They could travel days—weeks—without seeing another human being...if they could even survive that long.

They'd fled with nothing but the clothes on their backs. They had no food. No safe, filtered water, not even a water bottle. No way to find shelter to protect them from the elements and the deadly predators that called the Glades home—gators, snakes, boars, panthers.

She wished she'd been able to plan, to prepare, be ready—but they were running for their lives. She couldn't go back and change things now.

"I didn't bring us out here to die," Dakota whispered between clenched teeth. "I didn't."

23

DAKOTA

Dakota's eyes remained closed, deep within her memories. Trespassing on that man's property had been a dangerous proposition, but it beat dying of starvation, heat stroke, a venomous snake bite, or a gator's jaws.

She'd had no choice.

A dozen yards ahead, the channel was blocked by felled tree limbs. She cut the motor.

Dense cypress trees tangled overhead. The water looked black. Something heavy moved on the muddy bank and slipped into the water with a splash.

Against her legs, she felt Eden shudder, the knobs of her spine digging into Dakota's shins.

She used the pole to push the airboat up against the rotting dock that could have been there for fifty years. Maybe a hundred. Several boards were missing; those still intact were warped and moldy.

She helped Eden clamber over the aluminum side, the boat rocking with their every movement.

Eden moaned, making a strange, rasping sound. Dakota hitched her shoulder beneath Eden's arm, hissing as pain scorched her back, but she had to keep Eden on her feet.

They hurried along the dock until it ended abruptly, and their feet sank into mud so deep it sucked at their ankles.

An old shack on concrete blocks sagged ahead of them. It was nothing but old plywood covered in black tar paper. The door to the derelict cabin hung open like a gaping maw.

Inside, it was pitch black. She scanned the room with the flashlight—roaches and rats scurried from the light. More warped wood, mold, animal scat, and a raccoon carcass in the corner.

A table made out of two sawhorses and a split and peeling chunk of plywood. Three rusty metal chairs, one fallen on its side. And a cracked, blackened porcelain sink set into an unfinished wooden counter.

Half the ceiling had caved in over a filthy mattress shoved against the far wall. There was nothing for them here.

No food. No water. No shelter.

Eden's whole body quivered in terror. She held both hands to the shirt tied around her throat. Dakota was terrified to look, to see how bad it truly was.

"This isn't it," she said. "We're gonna find something better, I promise you."

She remembered what Maddox had said about the old man hiding his place in plain sight.

This was a decoy cabin, meant to make people think no one lived here anymore. His real place was further in.

She wrestled Eden's sagging body beneath her arm, her lower back aching, her muscles straining, the searing pain from the burn radiating from her shoulder up to her neck and down to her spine.

Wincing, she backed out of the cabin.

Her flashlight beam swept the darkness. Behind them, the water splashed—a fish, a turtle, or a gator. An owl hooted, a few birds calling in the night.

Something rustled to her left.

Her lungs constricted. She whipped the light around, staggering beneath her sister's weight.

Grunting, snuffling sounds filtered from the underbrush only ten feet away. A pair of eyes glowed back at her about two feet off the ground. She caught a glimpse of silvered tusks.

A boar.

Dakota went absolutely still.

Boars could be aggressive. Their tusks could do serious damage.

She had no weapons, no way to defend them. There was nowhere to run.

Maybe the airboat? Maybe, but the boar would reach them before they took more than a few steps. The boat was useless to them now.

She waited, not breathing, her pulse a roar in her skull.

Finally, the creature turned and shuffled off into the night.

She released a relieved breath. Ice water drained from her veins. She squeezed Eden's trembling shoulder. "We're okay, now. We're okay."

They were far from okay. Dakota was faint with hunger, thirst, pain, and terror. She couldn't stop her own shaking hands, blood still embedded beneath her fingernails, the cracks in her palms.

She closed her eyes against the fresh memory, sharp as coppery blood in her mouth: the wide, staring eyes, the spreading puddle beneath the body, not red like she'd expected, but an eerie, oily black.

And the rising desperate scream clawing up her own throat...

She blinked the terrible vision away. She couldn't lose it now.

Eden was hurt; she still didn't know how badly. They needed to find this guy's place. They needed food and water and rest.

Then she saw it. The overgrown trail wasn't even a trail— barely a divot in the stand of cypress trees.

She stared into the darkness, the dark tangle of trunks and vines, her heart thumping, the burn pulsing like a second heartbeat.

"This way," she whispered to Eden.

She barely remembered the frantic journey through the darkness, their skirts constantly caught on twigs, branches, and thorns, the spooky night sounds of raccoons screeching at each other, an owl hooting and another answering, creatures rustling through the brush on either side of them.

Mosquitoes whined around her face, biting through her clothes, any inch of exposed skin, even her eyelids. Eden stumbled beside her, silent but suffering, Dakota yanking her back to her feet again and again.

Something tangled around her leg.

She went down, taking Eden with her. Pain bit deep into her right calf. Barbed wire snarled around her leg, the barbs piercing her bare skin.

The flashlight flailed wildly as she took in the electrified fence topped by coils of barbed wire, a three-foot length of it downed by a felled tree, probably taken out by the huge storm the night before.

"Look, Eden. It's a sign." A sign from who, she didn't care, as long as it helped Eden.

She took several steadying breaths and pulled herself free of the barbed wire, hissing through clenched teeth at the stabs of pain.

Slick blood leaked over her fingers. She wiped them on her filthy skirt. The raw, boiled welt on her back burned. Every muscle in her back, arms, and legs ached.

Pain was a thing to endure. At least she had plenty of practice.

Carrying Eden's full weight, she scaled the fallen trunk and fell to the ground on the other side of the fence, nearly collapsing beneath the girl.

Dakota turned off the flashlight. They slipped through the darkness as silently as they could. Ahead of them, the moonlight revealed a one-story cabin in the center of a wide clearing flanked by several smaller buildings and a well.

Nothing special at first glance.

But Dakota remembered Maddox's warning. She hadn't forgotten the electrified fence. Anyone who chose to live out in the middle of the Glades all alone wasn't someone to be trifled with.

And yet, they had to risk it.

"Careful now," she warned both Eden and herself, well aware of the danger they were in.

Her throat was raw and burning with thirst. She was dizzy with hunger and pain.

"We get in, grab what we can take, and get out. There's a driveway on the other end of this property, a driveway that leads to a road that will get us away to someplace safe, okay?"

Eden hadn't nodded or shown she'd even heard Dakota. She had stared at the ground, rocking on her heels in exhaustion, her shoulders quaking.

Going into shock, maybe.

Fear constricted her throat, cutting off her breath. She'd seized Eden's shoulders and peered into her slack face. "I'm taking care of you, you hear me? You're my responsibility. I won't let you die, I swear to you. I won't leave you. Never, ever."

She'd kept her word back then.

She could do it again. She would do it again.

Now as she folded the drawing and slipped it carefully back into her pocket, Dakota repeated the words like a chant, an incantation, a promise. "I won't leave you. Never, ever."

24

LOGAN

"Hungry?" Logan held out an orange bag of Sun Chips and a bottle of water.

Dakota was dozing, her legs tucked up in the upholstered theater seat, her arms folded against her stomach, hidden. She looked small and vulnerable, a word he hadn't associated with the girl before now.

But the second he spoke, her eyes snapped open and she jumped to her feet, the knife already in her hand aimed at his chest.

A wary girl. And smart.

It was never a good idea to disarm an assailant with a knife unless you wanted to get stuck like a pincushion.

He took a step back, arms raised, the bag of chips, bottle of water, and a flashlight in his hands, an easy smile on his face. "Just thought you might be ready for some fuel."

He expected her to apologize or show a bit of embarrassment at pulling a knife on someone, but she merely shrugged. She didn't sheath the knife, either. "Sure."

He dropped the bag of chips and the water into her free hand.

She stretched and then settled back in the chair, placing the knife on the armrest beside her within easy reach. She scanned the auditorium with her flashlight.

The rest of the survivors were sleeping fitfully in various seats, most of them together near the front screen, which seemed to watch over them all like an enormous white eye.

Schmidt sat cross-legged in front of the food and water, his clipboard on his lap, pen in hand, still stubbornly awake. Of course he was.

"I'm Logan, by the way."

"I know."

He scanned the aisles and the rear of the theater for anything out of place, any potential threats, then sank down into the seat beside her. It was a habit now, ingrained in his DNA.

Dakota flashed him a guarded look, but didn't say anything.

"You've got a watch. It's analog, isn't it? I can't remember the last time I saw one of those."

She popped a chip into her mouth. "It was a gift."

"Good thing. It's the only way we'll know enough time has passed. What time is it, anyway?"

She glanced down, her face taut in the shadows. "Nine thirty-three a.m."

It'd been twenty-one hours since the bomb went off. How quickly everything could change. It only took a second for the world to go to hell.

Of course, he already knew that.

"First day of the end of the world," he quipped.

"Do you think so? The end of the world?"

He wanted to make a stupid joke, but the blast had shaken him, whether he wanted to admit it or not. "Not the world, maybe. But probably our country."

She chewed thoughtfully for a moment. "Everyone else

expects things to go back to normal within a week or two. I mean, I think they instinctively understand this is a worse terrorist attack than nine-eleven, but they think people will just go back to their homes, their jobs, that the infrastructure, this country as they know it, will hold.

"It won't. Not with multiple bombs killing hundreds of thousands of people. What if there are more bombs? Add in the fallout eradicating hundreds, maybe thousands of square miles of urban real estate for years?

"Millions of refugees without work, housing, or food and water. FEMA utterly overwhelmed. In huge swaths of the country, the infrastructure could simply collapse."

It was a sobering thought. Not that he wasn't used to a certain level of chaos, of lawlessness. But he'd put that life behind him, and he wasn't planning on going back. *But you kept the gun*, a voice whispered in his head. *You'll never change who you really are...*

"You thought it was coming, too," he said to push the ugly thoughts from his head. "That there were more bombs. That Miami could be a target. You knew right away."

"If you're always prepared for the worst, nothing can take you by surprise."

"Words to live by. That should be embroidered on a pillow or something."

She took a swig of water without looking at him. "You seem plenty prepared yourself."

He tensed. "How so?"

"Just a hunch. Those scars on your knuckles. The way you carry yourself."

He glanced at her again. She was observant, more so than the general population. Maybe too observant.

"You a soldier? Ex-military?"

"Something like that," he mumbled.

He hated that question. Hated everything it signified about what he wasn't, hated that it dredged up the shameful, whispering voices in his head.

A soldier was honorable. He was something else.

"Nice tats." She was looking at his arms, at the inked crosses, the snake winding through a skull across his left bicep, the large Virgin Mary gazing beatifically out at the world on his right.

Her gaze dropped to the Latin inscription tangled in the barbed wire on his forearm. Before she could ask what it meant, he shifted and moved his arm, blocking the inscription.

It was the last thing he wanted to discuss.

He was thirsty. But not for water.

The burning, *wanting* sensation had started last night. The desire building as a headache pounding at the base of his skull, as acid in the back of his throat.

He pulled his silver flask from the side pocket of his pants, grateful once again for his own foresight. He always kept it full— he never knew when he'd need a bit of calm, an oasis in the desert of his life.

Liquor wasn't always a refrigerator or bartender away.

He'd been drinking a sip or two every hour, displaying impressive levels of self-control, considering a literal bomb had just exploded his life.

It'd been enough to stave off the thirst, but he felt it now, stronger than ever.

He tilted his head back and gulped the last few precious swallows. His heart steadied as the sweet burn slid down his throat.

She cocked her brows at him.

"You see anything better to do?"

She didn't answer, just took another small sip of her water and capped it. It was still two-thirds full. She was conserving it.

"You got family to get back to?" he asked as a distraction. He wasn't used to this quiet stillness with no TV, no phone or radio, no hum of traffic or work business, no buzz of liquor in his blood to fill him with the warm nothingness he desired above all else.

It made him restless and anxious. He hated it.

For a few moments, she didn't answer. He started to think she was giving him the cold shoulder so he would leave.

He stared down at his empty flask, willing himself to get up and leave her to her peace, but some part of him simply didn't want to.

There was a wariness in her eyes, something haunted that he recognized in himself. Something broken in her, but also a strength like steel.

She'd kept her head in a disaster that felled most people. She'd gotten them here, after all.

"A sister," she said finally. "She's only fifteen. We're all we've got. She's waiting for me. She needs me."

"No parents? No other family?"

There was the slightest hesitation. "No."

"Me either." He flipped the flask and rubbed the grinning skull embossed on the side. He should probably feel depressed that he had no family to worry after, but he didn't. The fewer burdens to weigh one down, the better.

He'd never known who his father was—just a sperm donor in a long line of one-night stands, his strung-out mother willing to trade anything for her next fix. She was somewhere in Richmond, Virginia.

With a start, he wondered if she was still alive. Probably not.

She'd been a crack addict from his youngest memories, emaciated, shaky, with those hollow, desperate eyes—unable to keep a job, an apartment, or her own kid.

He'd left home at sixteen and never looked back. If that made him an asshole, then so be it.

He'd done worse things to survive. Much worse.

He slipped the flask back in his pocket. "You gonna stay here for a whole week?"

"I can't wait that long. The majority of the fallout will be gone after forty-eight hours."

"But not all of it."

"I'm still going," she said flatly. Her tone left no room for discussion.

"To each his own." What did he care what a stranger chose to do with her life? If she wanted to sacrifice it trying to find one person in the midst of a ruined, burning city, that was on her.

If this sister of hers was anywhere near the blast, she was probably already dead.

But he didn't need to tell her that. She already knew. He could see it in the way she clenched the bottle of water in both hands, her knuckles white.

A sudden noise drew their attention.

The doors to the auditorium—blocked from their view by the side wall along the stairs leading down to the main level—burst open with a loud, strident clang.

25
LOGAN

Logan was on his feet in an instant, instinctively feeling for the pistol at his back. He didn't want to draw if he didn't have to, but he was ready.

Dakota pushed past him and bounded down the stairs, her dark auburn hair streaming behind her.

Flashlight bobbing wildly, he leaped down the stairs after her. Most of the others were still sleeping, but a few raised their heads groggily, looking around for the source of the noise.

He and Dakota rounded the half-wall between the seats and the hallway leading to the double exit doors.

Red-headed Travis stood in the shadows. His freckles stood out on his pale skin like drops of blood. "I was using the restroom," he stammered. "I heard a noise in the foyer. This guy was stumbling around out there..."

Logan and Dakota focused their flashlights behind Travis. A man had entered through the double doors.

He staggered down the narrow hallway toward the main auditorium. He was nothing more than a lumbering shadow—thick and hunch-shouldered.

"Stay right there!" Logan shouted. "No closer."

The man sagged against the wall, his breathing labored and ragged.

Logan sucked in his own breath.

The man looked like something out of a horror movie. He was possibly Caucasian. It was impossible to tell even though he was nearly naked, only a few shreds of charred clothing hanging off him in tatters.

He was a mass of scorched flesh. The skin of his back and legs was burnt and blackened, the plaid pattern of the shirt he'd been wearing seared into the flabby folds of his chest and stomach.

Vomit stained the corners of his mouth. His face was misshapen. A nasty gash carved down the right side of his face, and red, weeping sores oozed on his forehead, cheeks, and chin.

The hair on the right side of his skull had burned completely off; on the left side, a raw, bare scalp shone through a few wispy clumps of brown hair.

He stank of urine and feces. A fetid, poisonous odor oozed from his every pore.

His blood-shot eyes gazed up at them with animal desperation. "H-help me."

Several others crowded into the hall space between the doors and the auditorium, though they remained a safe distance away.

Rasha covered her mouth and nose with her hands, eyes wide with horror. "What happened to him?"

"The bomb happened to him," Dakota said. She didn't back away or cover her face, but her voice trembled. "The radiation."

"The poor man." Shay stood beside Rasha and offered her arm for support. "I've seen black-and-white pictures in textbooks, but nothing like this…"

Miles' sunburned face blanched. His gaze flicked from the burned man to Dakota. "It—it really was a nuke."

Dakota said nothing. Neither did Logan.

There was nothing to say.

For a terrible moment, everyone simply stared at the man in appalled disbelief.

This would've happened to them if they hadn't found shelter. That's what they were all thinking, the horror of the bomb finally sinking in, finally taking hold.

The horror still happening out there to thousands of people, to people they knew, to friends and family members, to daughters and sons and girlfriends and husbands and parents.

Logan had seen his share of horror.

But this was something else. This was heinous, an unspeakable tragedy on a catastrophic scale.

Rasha whimpered. Shay pressed her fist to her mouth. Isabel collapsed against her grandmother, who wrapped her thin, veiny arms around the girl and wept silently.

"It's real," Miles muttered to himself. "It's really real."

"We have to help him," Julio said.

"Is he...contagious?" Rasha asked.

"No," Shay said shakily. "Radiation poisoning isn't contagious, but his clothes and skin are likely covered in radioactive particles. Don't touch him."

"We need to keep him here in the hallway," Dakota said grimly, "so he doesn't contaminate the auditorium."

"Water..." the man groaned.

Dakota gestured to Travis, who still stood frozen, his hands hanging limp at his sides, his pale face slack with shock. "You heard him. Bring him some water."

Travis moved to obey, but Schmidt seized his arm. He glared at Dakota as if she alone had brought this calamity upon him. "That man is dying, isn't he?"

Shay answered, "This is—he's suffering from acute radiation syndrome."

"Look at him!" Schmidt spoke like the man couldn't hear them. "He's knocking at death's door. It's a miracle he stayed on his feet long enough to make it here."

"He needs immediate medical attention," Shay stammered, glancing at the injured man. She was trying to be compassionate, but they all saw it. Schmidt was right. It was a miracle the guy was even breathing.

"Which he's not gonna get," Schmidt scoffed. "We can't afford to waste anything. We need to save that water for the living."

"Give him the water," Dakota repeated.

"I thought we had to ration and conserve everything to survive. Isn't that what *she* insisted?" He jabbed a finger at Dakota.

Logan watched the drama unfold impassively. He was a little surprised at her. She'd seemed so tough and logical, but this was a merciful choice, not a rational one.

It seemed simple enough—what was one water bottle, after all?

But what about when the man lasted for hours or days, and one bottle turned into ten or twenty or more?

In a situation like this, survival had to win every time.

"Take one from my share," Julio said quietly.

"No," Schmidt insisted. "I'm in charge of the supplies. I decide who gets what. We all feel sorry for him, but it's useless to waste—"

"Hot," the man moaned. "So hot...water, please..."

Dakota's mouth tightened. She whirled on Schmidt with a baleful glare. "If you don't give this man water right now, so help me, but I'll make you regret it."

Schmidt gave a smug sneer. He balled his hands into fat,

fleshy fists. "Just who do you think you are? What makes you think you get to make decisions for the whole group? You're just a stupid girl who doesn't know when to keep her mouth shut."

Dakota stalked up to him, indignant.

For a second, Logan thought she was going to deck the idiot like he deserved.

Instead, she strode past him along the right side of the hallway, aiming for the bottled waters stacked against the far wall of the auditorium.

Schmidt seized her arm. "What did I just tell you—"

But he never finished his sentence.

Dakota dropped her flashlight. In one fluid movement, she grabbed the man's shoulders and jerked him toward her while simultaneously thrusting her leg up, kneeing him in the groin so hard he collapsed to the carpet.

Schmidt let out a sharp, agonized *Ugh*. He curled into a ball, groaning and clutching his crotch. "You little—!"

"You're welcome." Dakota stepped over him, retrieved her flashlight, and grabbed a water from the stack.

As she walked back to the wounded man, her eyes met Logan's, her gaze fierce, daring him to object.

He nodded at her in acknowledgment, impressed yet again. She was tougher than she looked.

Schmidt wheezed out a nasty insult.

"Not cool, man," Julio said. "There's no reason to be like that."

"This is my theater!" Schmidt cried, furious tears leaking down his heavy cheeks. "You have no right! Get out! You freeloading troublemakers better leave, right now—"

"We aren't going anywhere." Logan squatted down next to Schmidt and cracked his knuckles. He didn't need to threaten. His presence was enough.

Logan was an easygoing guy. The less he cared about

anything, the better off he was. But a pissant attacking women, verbal or otherwise, was just one of those things. The fat, squirming fool deserved whatever he got.

"Here's what you're gonna do for the next week," he said. "You're going to sit here and shut up. You're not gonna bother with anybody here. Not her, not Julio, and certainly not me. Tell me we understand each other."

The guy only moaned.

Logan smiled. "Close enough."

Dakota handed the water to Shay, who knelt in front of the burned man and offered him a drink, careful not to touch him.

He slurped it down greedily, desperately, water dribbling over his blistered lips.

"Th-thank you," the man rasped.

"I'm sorry we don't have more medical supplies," Shay said, her voice cracking with unshed tears. "We ran out. You need sterile dressings, intravenous antibiotics, a morphine drip..."

"My head," the man said, "feels like it's splitting open."

"I have Tylenol in my purse," Zamira offered. She disentangled herself from Isabel and Piper, who were both clutching at her, and handed Shay a small bottle of pills.

She gave the man half a dozen pills, hesitated, then offered him several more. "I hope this helps a little."

"What's it like out there?" Julio asked.

The man swallowed the last of the pills. He touched the mottled, burned side of his face with trembling fingers. "Hell."

26

LOGAN

Logan forced himself not to look away in revulsion. The man looked like hell itself.

"Do you—do you know who did this?" Rasha asked tremulously. "Have you heard any news?"

The man shook his head, his eyes half-closed. He groaned from the pain. Sweat beaded his mottled forehead. "Damn Muslims. Never should've let them sand maggots into our country."

Rasha stiffened.

Logan went tense. "Have you heard anything on the emergency broadcasts? Something concrete with actual evidence?"

"Don't need to be told—what's plain to see," the man forced out. "We already know—who did this."

"You think it was ISIS?" Schmidt asked.

"No—" The man turned his head and vomited. Bloody spittle dribbled from his swollen lips. "All of 'em."

"That's not true," Shay said.

Logan said, "We don't know anything."

"There are bad apples in every group of human beings on the

planet," Dakota said through gritted teeth. "Yeah, ISIS and all the radicals like them are evil as hell, but it doesn't make all Muslims bad."

He lifted one burned arm with great effort, wincing from the pain, and pointed at Rasha. "You—you did this to us!"

Rasha flinched.

Shay reared back, gaping. "I'm sure you don't mean that. You're in incredible pain—"

"I mean...just what I said! We should've killed 'em all in Iraq—"

"Enough!" Anger sparked through Logan. He restrained the sudden urge to slug the guy, dying or not. Or at least stick a roll of duct tape over his mouth.

He and Dakota exchanged a hard glance. The guy was suffering, about to die, but that didn't excuse his racist bullshit.

As a Colombian, Logan had heard plenty of similar crap—noxious, hate-filled insults hurled at him because of his skin tone, his heritage.

He rubbed his scarred knuckles and took a step back, fighting back the anger.

That wasn't who he was, not anymore.

"You should rest and save your energy," Julio said diplomatically. "We'll make you as comfortable as we can."

"Now look what's happened..." the guy continued as if he hadn't heard Julio. He grimaced. Blood leaked down his neck in sickly red-brown rivulets. "Look what they've done to us..."

The man turned his head to the side and vomited violently. He retched, his eyes rolling wildly, his ravaged body convulsing. Eventually, he sank into unconsciousness.

Logan let out a relieved sigh. Not even racist asshats deserved a death like this, but Logan wasn't going to shed any tears for him, either.

"This is my country, too," Rasha said in a soft, strained voice. She touched her hijab self-consciously. "I love America and the freedom it stands for. No true, peace-loving Muslim would ever do such a thing or ever condone it."

She blinked rapidly, looking rattled but trying to regain her composure. Miles, to his credit, stood beside her and rubbed her shoulders to reassure and comfort her.

"We know that," Julio said kindly. "We understand that ISIS and their ilk are a corruption. They're no more Muslim than the Ku Klux Klan are Christians."

Rasha gave Julio a nod, the tension in her face easing slightly. Miles squeezed his wife's shoulders.

"What about North Korea?" Walter growled. "Kim Jong-un is crazy enough to kill us all and destroy his own damn country just for spite."

"Could be," Dakota allowed, though a line appeared between her brows. "It's possible. Could be a terrorist group we've never heard of. Maybe even domestic."

"I bet it's the Russians," Walter said with a derisive sniff. "They've always hated America."

"My dad says Putin wants to take over our country, just like the Nazis," Travis said.

Logan scratched his chin. "Our military is prepared for that. And those governments know we'd strike back with enough fury to wipe them off the map."

"Dakota's hunch is the most likely, I think," Logan said. "An IND fabricated by a terrorist group or a rogue nation."

"How the hell could terrorists get a hold of nuclear material?" Miles shook his head in disbelief. "It's gotta be a rogue state."

"They could build one from the components of a stolen weapon," Logan said, "or one they bought from black market arms dealers. Once they have the nuclear material—plutonium or highly enriched uranium—it's not hard to make the bomb."

"How can you be so sure it's not Russia or China?" Travis asked.

"Russia, China, or another country could still be behind this," Julio said. "They could've made it look like terrorists to avoid payback—mutually assured destruction."

"It's possible, but it doesn't really make sense." Logan pulled out his flask and shook it. Damn. Still empty.

"If a superpower is behind this," he said, "their first priority would be to destroy their adversary's ability to fight back. They'd target our inter-continental ballistic missiles, nuclear submarine bases, our airfields housing nuclear bombers. Cities will be last on the list—especially Miami."

"If it *is* ISIS or some other terrorist group, what could they be targeting?" Shay asked.

Logan shoved the flask in his back pocket with a resigned sigh. "Anything. Could be military bases, oil refineries, large military industrial manufacturing facilities.

"Major ports or transportation hubs. Economic and industrial facilities, power generation. Or large cities, for maximum casualties, to inflict horrendous damage to morale."

"I don't understand." Shay hugged herself, clearly rattled. "How could people hate us so much?"

Dakota gave a dismissive wave of her hand. "It doesn't matter right now."

Shay lifted her chin. "It matters to me."

Dakota scowled. "Of course it does, in the long run. But now? Right now, we have to live. And if you want to live, you've got to focus on what you need to do right here, right now. Understand?"

"Dakota's right," Zamira said. "She is wise. As I always tell my grandchildren, worry only causes more wrinkles. It changes nothing."

"It's all just rumors until we get some actual concrete news," Logan said.

"It's a waste of energy," Dakota said. "Energy we need to survive."

Rasha wrung her hands. She glanced at the dying man and looked quickly away, aghast. "How does...how does the radiation *do* that to someone?"

"I remember some of this from my training." Shay sucked in a deep, steadying breath. When she spoke, her voice was calm. "He was exposed to thermal energy from proximity to the blast—over fifty percent of his body has sustained third- and second-degree burns. His clothes were—they were burned right off him.

"As for the radiation...nuclear radiation ionizes atoms by knocking off their electrons. The ionizing radiation damages DNA molecules by breaking the bonds between atoms.

"If radiation changes DNA molecules enough, cells can't replicate and begin to die. Less severely damaged cells may survive and replicate, but the structural changes in their DNA disrupt normal cell processes—cells that can't control their division grow out of control and become cancerous.

"That could take months, years, or decades. But the immediate concern is acute radiation syndrome."

"Could you break that down for us?" Julio asked. "What is happening—and what will happen—to all those people out there exposed to radiation?"

Shay grimaced, the light in her eyes dimming. "Medical personnel measure absorbed radiation in grays, like Dakota said. At one to two grays, acute radiation syndrome sets in with nausea, vomiting, and headaches.

"You'll have intense itching, redness like a sunburn, and blisters and ulcers. While the cancer rate goes up dramatically, most people will survive.

"But as the level of exposure increases, you'll lose your hair. You'll start bleeding beneath the skin, with infections and hemorrhaging."

Shay paused and took a steadying breath. "At six to eight grays, the stem cells in your bone marrow and the cells lining your GI tract are dying. Your circulatory system starts to collapse. Fever, diarrhea, and severe vomiting start almost right away.

"Seizures and coma will lead to death in fifty percent of patients within a few weeks, even with medical interventions such as bone marrow transplants."

"And beyond nine gray?" Logan asked.

Shay glanced at Isabel and Piper and chewed on her thumbnail, hesitating. "Well, the odds aren't very good."

"Give it to us straight," Logan said.

He needed to know exactly what he was up against. The odds had never been in his favor. Yet he'd still managed to beat them, time after time, even when a part of him would rather give in to defeat.

Shay met his gaze without flinching. "Everyone dies."

Murmurs of mingled dismay and relief filled the auditorium. Julio touched his gold cross. Zamira bowed her head and clutched her granddaughter's limp hand.

Shay glanced over at the unconscious man, her lips pursed. "It's only been twenty-four hours since the bomb. The level of radiation he's absorbed must be extremely high for the onset to be so severe so quickly.

"At least ten gray. Probably more. I doubt he'll live more than a day." Shay looked at Dakota, her eyes glassy with tears. "We're the lucky ones."

Logan hadn't felt lucky in a very long time. Maybe never. Luck had never played into it.

Life was a scrape for survival, doing what you have to do to get by, to endure until the next miserable, monotonous day.

But now, maybe for the first time, he felt the weight of something like luck settling on him.

He was still alive.

Someone who didn't deserve it. If he deserved anything, it was a bottomless pit, or maybe a hell of endless torture.

And yet here he was.

Lucky.

For today, at least.

27
MADDOX

Twenty yards ahead of Maddox, the door to a charred Jeep thrust open.

A dark shape fell out and climbed slowly to its feet. Its body was blackened from head to foot. Its hair was burned off. Black rags hung from its torso. And the face—white bulging eyes, mouth gaping open like a black pit—it was barely human.

The creature tottered toward him, arms outstretched, palms down like some sort of zombie. Maddox watched in stunned silence as the figure lunged at him.

Maddox stepped backward, toward the entrance to the tunnel. He didn't scream, though his heart jerked against his bruised ribcage.

The figure took one more staggering step and collapsed. Its body convulsed for a moment, then stilled.

It didn't move.

Maddox stared down at it, blinking rapidly.

He lifted his head slowly and looked around. He was alone on the causeway. If there had been others, they'd escaped or they were dead, like the pathetic creature lying at his feet.

His head hurt like someone had driven spikes through the center of his brain. Everything was thick and fuzzy. White spots flickered in front of his vision. His mind was jumbled with confusion, shock, and pain.

It took him a long moment to even recall his name. He'd blacked out and awoken to the crushed taxi, the collapsed tunnel. He remembered that.

He didn't know how long he'd been unconscious. Hours, it must've been. The sun had vanished from the sky.

The causeway shuddered beneath his feet. The water on either side looked dark and ominous, eager to swallow up a hundred thousand tons of concrete and steel if only given the chance.

It wasn't safe here.

Maddox left the body behind and began to walk. He didn't yet know what to do or where to go. Find a hospital, maybe. Escape this living hell.

There was no other way to go other than toward ground zero, at least for now. Behind him, the tunnel had collapsed in a hail of cement and twisted beams. Before him was the causeway leading to the mainland, the Atlantic Ocean far below.

He shuffled down the causeway, staggering past vehicles crushed, twisted, and smashed, their burned-out husks like metal skulls.

He moved into a world that had gone a flat and colorless gray. The air thickened with a burning, singed stench that clotted in his nostrils and clogged his throat.

The closer he got to downtown, the worse things became.

Fires from ruptured gas and downed power lines sprang to life. Smoke billowed into the blackened sky. Debris, rubble, and charred, broken palm trees lay everywhere.

All around him, buildings sagged as if their foundations were made of jelly. A forty-story steel building lay tossed like a child's toy in the bay, half-submerged, a smashed and twisted wreck of mangled girders.

Dozens of buildings had collapsed completely, spectacular feats of architecture now utterly destroyed, the rubble forming small, jagged mountains between the wrecked structures.

Bodies littered the sidewalk and streets, slumped in burning cars. The dust and ash hung so thick in the air. The living drifted about like shadowy ghosts. In some cases, he couldn't distinguish male from female, old from young.

Blisters marred their faces, their arms, their legs, some as large as tennis balls. Their skin erupted with angry burns, as if they'd been splashed with boiling water.

And then there were those burned and blackened like they'd been roasted alive. They moved slowly, arms outstretched, shuffling through the smoke. They walked as if in a numbed stupor, too shocked to react, to feel pain, to scream. Some were still clothed; some wore rags.

He watched an elderly woman stumbling down the sidewalk toward him. Her hair was gone. She was completely naked.

Behind her, others emerged from the smoke, their exposed bodies filmed in gray ash. The heat had burned their clothes away.

How could that be? How could any of this be?

A man brushed past him, his scorched arms outstretched to prevent the burns from touching any other part of himself. A twisted chunk of metal jutted from the man's neck. Blood pooled in the hollow of his collarbone and dripped down his charred chest.

The thought came to Maddox to warn the man that he was bleeding out, but no sound escaped his lips.

It was strange—he heard very little sound. No screaming. No crying. He couldn't wrap his fuzzy mind around what that meant.

A man sat on the curb, rocking back and forth as he peeled off seared shreds of his flesh from his arms. Others clutched at their ears, their eardrums ruptured from the pressure of the blast, their sooty faces contorted in agony.

A woman in her fifties drifted past him like a ghost. She clutched her stomach, blackened blood coating her hands as she held in her own intestines.

A girl of twelve or thirteen ran by, her hand over her left eye, blood leaking from the empty socket.

"What do we do?" a man cried, grasping Maddox's shirt and shaking his shoulders.

The man wore a lavender silk shirt beneath an expensive suit. The stench of burned flesh overwhelmed the strong scent of cologne. His face twisted with an animal terror.

Maddox shoved him away. He had no answers.

Even if he did, his only concern was for himself.

He stood in the center of the street, numb and stunned, ash and debris and chaos all around him. Something light and feathery brushed his arms, his face.

He looked up into the gloom. Something like sand was falling from the sky, fine granules mingled with the ash.

He flicked it off. More fell.

He did not understand fully what it meant.

Yet he knew on some deep, primal level, that the horror was just beginning.

28
DAKOTA

Day two passed much like the first: in quiet desperation. Unable to sleep or relax, Dakota counted the seconds, minutes, and hours on her watch. She ate a Mars bar, half a box of Nerds, and a few bags of chips.

At the twenty-four-hour mark, she washed her face and armpits and rinsed out her mouth. Already, her mouth felt grimy. She ran her tongue over her fuzzy teeth over and over, fantasizing about hot showers and electric toothbrushes.

Sometime around the thirty-six-hour mark, the wounded man died.

Julio and Zamira insisted on saying a prayer over the body, and then Logan and Julio carefully dragged him out of auditorium seven, into the room next door.

The other survivors huddled together, finding some remnant of hope and connection with each other, with human contact. Schmidt, sufficiently cowed, kept to himself.

So did Dakota.

Logan had become even more restless than she was. He spent

the hours pacing the aisles—first the left side, along the back, down the right aisle, across the front to begin again.

Several times, he took out his flask, shook it, and then returned it to his jeans pocket with a disgusted curse.

At the forty-six-hour mark, she couldn't bear to wait any longer. Her sister needed her desperately. She couldn't remain here much longer, helpless, utterly useless.

Dakota slipped down the narrow hallway unnoticed, her flashlight switched off, and eased through the auditorium's double doors.

The wide hallway lined with giant posters of upcoming movies was swathed in heavy shadows. She could barely make out enough detail to edge down the hallway to the large foyer area.

She passed the ticket counter and the concession stand. A dense, heavy gray light streamed through the shattered front doors. Was the sky simply cloudy, or was the radiation still falling?

It shouldn't be, but what did she know, really? All the research was based on extrapolations from Hiroshima and Nagasaki, government tests over oceans and deserts, and nuclear reactor accidents.

There had never been a large nuclear groundburst to study.

What if they were wrong?

Slowly and carefully, as if her caution could prevent contamination, she made her way to within ten yards of the entrance.

The world outside was as eerily empty and silent as it was inside the theater. In the parking lot, dozens of cars still sat where they'd been abandoned.

Fine-grained fallout covered the ground and blanketed the cars like silt. Shards of glass lay everywhere, glinting from the debris.

Three palm trees grew from a grassy island in the middle of the parking lot. She squinted, studying the palms, the way their fronds swayed and rustled. The breeze still blew to the north, maybe northwest. It was hard to tell.

If the prevailing winds blew the same direction the last two days, everything north of them was contaminated—and dangerous.

She needed to go northwest almost two and a half miles to reach her sister.

But after that, her destination was directly perpendicular to the swath of fallout. Once she and Eden traveled a few miles west, they'd be in the clear—west along Route 41, through the city and suburbs to the outskirts of civilization.

It was nearly the same path she and Eden had fled two years ago.

Of course, if the wind had changed to an easterly direction at any point, west wouldn't be safe either. She just had to hope her plan was sound.

She hated relying on hope and assumption, but she had no choice.

"This is the right thing," she said aloud. "It has to be."

She left the flashlight switched off and trudged back toward auditorium seven in darkness, exhausted but resolute. She opened the auditorium door.

A figure lunged out of the shadows.

Fear jolted through her.

Instinct took over. She seized her knife and jerked it from its sheath in one fluid, practiced movement. In half a second, she had the blade pressed against her assailant's neck. "Move and I slit your throat."

The figure stepped swiftly to the right. He slammed the side of his palm against her knife hand.

Before she could react with a counter move, her arm was thrust backward, pain exploding in her wrist. The knife dropped from her numb fingers.

He seized her arm and shoved it against the still opened door.

She hissed out a pained breath.

"You can try," Logan said.

Her pulse roared in her ears. The fear was in her, and she hated it. It made her furious. "Let go of me!"

He released her.

She stepped back, her heart stuttering, fear still pumping through her. The scars on her back burned.

Memories of shadows looming over her seared her mind. She blinked them away.

The fear she'd felt back then, the pain and rage and helplessness—it was the past. This was now.

She rubbed her bruised wrist and forced herself to take several deep, steady breaths before responding. The fear and adrenaline drained out of her, leaving her heavy-limbed and irritated—but at herself.

If he were a real enemy, she'd smash his knee or groin with a solid kick or claw at his eyeballs with her fingernails. She still half-wanted to. "Unless you have a death wish, in the future, you might avoid startling someone with a knife."

He shrugged. "You hesitated. Next time, don't give your target that window of opportunity. Stab hard and fast."

"You'd rather I killed you, then?"

His teeth flashed in the shadows. "Like I said, you can try."

"You'd be surprised what I can do with a knife," she snapped, both disgruntled and grudgingly impressed.

He sounded like Ezra. Just like she'd suspected, he knew his way around a fight. He knew exactly what he was doing.

A wry smile tugged at his lips. "I'd like to see that someday."

She bent down, retrieved her knife, and sheathed it. She

pulled out her flashlight and stepped around him without looking at him. "Sorry to disappoint you."

"You're leaving," he said to her back.

"I have to."

"What about the fallout?"

"It'll be forty-eight hours in less than sixty minutes. Radiation levels will be at one percent of the original dose. That's good enough for me."

She strode quickly down the hallway, leaving Logan Garcia behind.

29
DAKOTA

Dakota reached the front of the auditorium, where most of the survivors sat or slept near the screen wall.

Walter was curled in a corner, sleeping. Julio sat beside him, his head leaning back against the wall, his eyes closed. Schmidt guarded the food while Travis, Miles, and the teens stretched out on the raised-armrest seats.

Zamira, Rasha, Shay, and Piper were quietly playing a game of Monopoly Deal with cards Zamira had found in her voluminous purse. Rasha was sitting next to Piper. She'd taken an interest in the girl and helped Zamira care for her.

Piper was smiling. She was a tough, resilient little girl. She was going to make it.

Isabel, on the other hand, slumped cross-legged beside her grandmother, her hands limp on her lap, her eyes glassy and unfocused.

She needed to wake up and get a grip if she was going to survive in this dark new world. At least she had a good chance with a strong woman like Zamira looking after her.

Dakota had to worry about Eden now.

"I'm leaving," Dakota announced. "I'm headed north to get my sister, then west to escape the radiation contamination. I'm taking the risk. You should stay here for another five days to be safe. There will be more food without me."

"I'm going with you." Shay dropped her cards and pulled herself to her feet. She ran her hands through her thick, springy coils and straightened her shoulders. "Count me in."

Dakota shook her head. "It's still dangerous out there. If radiation levels were at a thousand rem two days ago, it's ten rem an hour now."

"That doesn't sound like much," Rasha said.

"Remember, it's cumulative. At ten rem an hour, you only have to spend ten to twenty hours in a contaminated area to reach acute radiation syndrome levels. And we weren't completely protected here. We've already absorbed a low dose. I can't say for sure how much."

Rasha made a fearful sound in the back of her throat. She looked up at the ceiling as if the radiation infiltrating the theater was visible to the naked eye.

Zamira patted her shoulder. "The safest place is to wait it out here for the full week, like Dakota said."

"What if we went south?" Miles asked. "What about the Keys? You said the radiation is only north."

"I said probably," Dakota corrected.

"The Keys will have their own troubles soon enough," Logan said as he came up next to her. He stretched lazily and scratched his scruffy jaw.

Dakota took a step away from him, tensing. She could still feel his shadow looming over her, his strong hand encircling her wrist.

She was irritated with herself and him—but it also gave her an inkling of an idea.

"What do you mean?" Miles asked.

"When the trucks don't come to stock up the stores and gas stations," Logan said, "what're they gonna do? They're surrounded on three sides by water, nowhere to go but north—and that's where the chaos is. Seems like they're in for a world of hurt in a few days, if it hasn't started already."

"It sounds like a lot of places are in for a world of hurt," Julio said soberly.

Shay chewed on her thumbnail, her expression troubled. "We don't know that. Not for sure."

"Okay, fine. We don't know for sure. We don't know anything for sure. But we'll find out, won't we?"

Dakota turned away from the group. She didn't feel much like talking.

Her stomach rumbled. She didn't want to take more food that Zamira and Piper and the others would need later, but she needed sustenance for the journey ahead.

One. She'd take just one item and leave the rest to give everyone the best chance of survival. The longer they remained inside, the safer they would be.

She strode over to the food supply and grabbed a bag of Doritos, ignoring Schmidt's baleful glare. She retreated to her usual spot in the rear of the auditorium to wait out the next hour.

Her gaze snagged on Logan, who was back to pacing the far side aisle.

He climbed the left set of stairs, strode along the upper back row of seats, descended the right stairs, walked back and completed the circuit again, restless as a tiger.

In the semi-dark, she couldn't make out the shape of the pistol tucked snugly against his back beneath his loose T-shirt, but she knew it was there.

She needed her own gun. It wasn't safe out there. A knife was only good for quick and dirty attacks and close-quarters ambushes.

It wouldn't be enough. Not with thousands of terrified, wounded people stumbling about—dazed, helpless, and devastated. After forty-eight hours without water, they'd be desperate, willing to do just about anything to get food and drink for their children, for themselves.

She knew how easily the civilized veneer slid off a person as soon as the doors were closed, as soon as they needed or wanted something badly enough.

She had the scars, didn't she?

Dakota suppressed a shudder. It wasn't just the chaos of desperate survivors she feared. The back of her neck prickled, apprehension pooling in her stomach.

Maddox was still out there.

She longed to assume he was dead, to be done with it and rid herself of him once and for all.

Tens of thousands of people had been incinerated in the blink of an eye. Why not Maddox? He deserved it more than any of them.

But she knew better. That was too easy. Not a single thing in her entire life had ever been easy.

Maddox was still alive, still hunting.

She had to be ready. She couldn't afford to underestimate him, to let him take her by surprise again.

She clenched her jaw, considering the options.

She didn't like the obvious choice, the one building in the back of her mind.

But she didn't have a lot of choices. The walls were closing in on her, an enormous weight bearing down on her chest. She needed something from Logan Garcia, whether she liked it or not.

She sucked in a sharp breath. *Here goes nothing.*

30
DAKOTA

Dakota rose from her seat, strode across the center aisle, and approached Logan. "You should sell me your gun."

He stopped, his foot hovering over the next stair for a moment. He took a step down and turned to face her. "What gun?"

They were separated by six stairs. She gazed steadily up at him. "I know a concealed carry when I see it. You've got a compact pistol in an inside-the-waistband holster at the small of your back."

He scratched at his scruffy jawline, hesitating. Maybe he was deciding whether to admit it. Some people freaked out in the presence of a gun, but she wasn't one of them.

He gave a lazy shrug. "You can never be too careful these days."

"I don't disagree. Which is why I'll buy it off you."

This time, he didn't hesitate. "Not a chance."

"I have a hundred bucks on me."

He laughed mirthlessly.

"Fine. Two hundred."

"No deal."

"Five hundred," she lied.

"I'll take a hard pass." He cocked a wry eyebrow. "Doubt you've got that kind of cash on you, anyway."

She hadn't thought it would work, but anything was worth a shot.

Briefly, she considered rushing him, grabbing the gun, and running. But that was stupid.

She'd bet that five hundred bucks that this guy was ex-military. He seemed reticent about discussing anything personal, but she saw it in every movement of his muscled, well-honed body.

He was a fighter, a warrior.

Ezra had taught her some skills, but she was nothing if not self-aware. This wasn't flabby, pretentious Schmidt, easy to take down with a well-placed kick.

Logan Garcia wasn't someone to be messed with.

Which was why she needed him.

"Come with me, then. I could use someone who knows what they're doing."

"Who says I know what I'm doing?"

"Enough with the games. I can tell you know your way around a fight."

He gave a sour laugh. "I don't fight. My main pastime is drinking. I'm very good at it."

She didn't believe that for a hot second. "You keep a gun on you, but you don't fight?"

He cracked his battle-scarred knuckles. "Not anymore."

"But you know how."

"You could say that."

"Like I said, you don't want to sell me your gun, fine. Then come with me."

He leaned against the wall, crossed his arms, and gave her a cool, assessing look. "Why would I wanna go out there? You basically told everyone they'd end up like the overcooked dead guy."

"I exaggerated a bit." She didn't know if she had. Likely, she hadn't.

She guessed the exposure outside was still between five and ten rem an hour. They'd succumb to radiation sickness in less than twenty-four hours of exposure.

If the blast was larger than ten kilotons or closer than she'd estimated, it could be higher. And instead of vomiting and diarrhea, they'd be dealing with seizures and comas.

But there was no way to know until they got sick or made it to a hospital. Every working hospital within a hundred miles must be overwhelmed by now.

She despised this not-knowing, so many lives depending on guesswork and supposition.

She wanted facts. Knowledge.

It was what they didn't know that would kill them.

She loathed speaking the words, but she forced herself to say them anyway. This wasn't about her; it was about Eden. And for Eden, she'd do anything.

She cleared her throat. "I—I need your help."

He studied her for a moment, eyebrows raised.

"I'm going north to get my sister, then west to escape the chaos. It's dangerous out there, especially alone. I could use someone who has my back. Just for a few days."

"What makes you think I'd be interested in helping you?"

"Because you're going stir-crazy in here. It's driving you mad, I can see it."

He ran his hand through his black, disheveled hair and shook his head. "I'm right as rain. Free rent? Free food? I'm good."

"No, you aren't. And neither am I. I'm getting out of this damn city. I know you want to go, too."

"So, go."

"Not without my sister."

"That's not my problem." Logan snorted and turned away. He headed up the stairs. "Enjoy your trip."

She stared at his retreating back, at the bulge of his weapon, a weapon she needed, until her eyes blurred. She didn't want to trust him. She didn't trust anyone.

But she knew what it would be like out there. Ezra had warned her. People wounded and sick, hungry and desperate. Their baser, brutal animal instincts would show themselves soon, if they hadn't already.

She knew better than anyone what desperate people were capable of.

And there was Maddox.

She about choked on the word. "Please."

He didn't turn around.

Fear speared her. She could not, under any circumstances, underestimate that man. If he found them and she had nothing but a knife to defend them, Eden was already lost. And Dakota was already dead.

She was going to have to give up something important to snare Logan.

An image of Ezra popped into her head: bent over the wooden kitchen table intent on cleaning one of his rifles; that grizzled, white-whiskered face scored with wrinkles; those bright, intelligent sky-blue eyes.

She knew exactly where they needed to go.

She had no interest in taking any of the others there. They had their own families, the pieces of their own lives to try and pick up after they left the auditorium.

She'd gotten them to shelter, saved them from the fallout. That was enough. Besides, outside was a dangerous place to be right now. She didn't want Zamira or the girls out there, vulnerable and exposed.

Only Dakota would go. And Logan, if she could convince him.

It felt like a betrayal, offering something that wasn't hers to give. Ezra wouldn't understand. He'd hate her for it.

Maybe he wouldn't even let them in.

She ran her tongue over her bottom lip, thinking, considering, weighing the costs and benefits. She lowered her voice. "I know a place. A safehouse."

He stopped. "Why would I need a safehouse?"

Logan turned and stared down at her with that dark, level gaze of his. It felt like he could see all the way into the back of her head, could pick apart her thoughts, her memories, her fears.

Ezra had a look like that, too. She'd hated it.

"Because you're not stupid. You know everything's collapsing. Our infrastructure can't possibly handle a million dead and a million more fatally wounded. What about the millions of displaced, homeless, and hungry people?

"How is Miami going to get fuel? Fresh water? Food? How is Fort Lauderdale? Or Homestead and the Keys? Even if the National Guard or FEMA comes with supplies, how long is it going to take to get down here?

"You know as well as I do that we're on our own, at least for a while. For the next several weeks at least, the only safe places are ones with razor-wired walls and electrified fences and three years' worth of stored food and supplies. You personally know of any bunkers like that?"

He didn't say anything.

"My friend owns a place. Off the grid, with a well and solar electricity. He'll take us in—you too," she lied.

Even as she spoke, the plan shifted in her mind. She didn't

have to worry about Ezra taking Logan in if she never brought him to the cabin in the first place.

She didn't owe this guy a thing. There was no reason she had to keep her promise. She could use him to get to the Tamiami Trail, then find a way to lose him. In the chaos, it'd be easy.

Dakota was no stranger to lying through her teeth. And she was damn good at it.

"You'll be safe." She gave him a wide, genuine smile. "I guarantee it."

His expression remained impassive. But he hadn't said no again. She took that as a good sign.

"You said yourself you have no family to weigh you down. You don't have an apartment left to go back to. No job. Face it. You've got nothing."

He snorted. "Thanks for the pep talk."

"Help me get my sister. I'll take you to the safehouse. Then you can decide to stay or go. You can hole up for a few weeks until the power comes back on and FEMA gets their act together.

"Or, if you decide you'd rather go, we'll give you supplies and as much whiskey as you can carry."

His eyebrows shot up.

"That's right. My friend likes his booze as much as I suspect you do. He's got a three-year supply of that, too."

"Just what kind are we talking about here?"

"Beer, whiskey, tequila, vodka, gin. Whatever you want, he's got it."

He cracked his knuckles one by one, his face unreadable. Then something shifted in his expression. That easy grin returned, though it never reached his eyes. "Just where is this mythical place?"

She smiled, knowing the battle was already won. "The Everglades."

31
EDEN

Eden lost track of time. Every so often, she got out of the tub, crawled across the cool tile floor, hand outstretched until she touched the door, and moved the towel she'd shoved against the crack in the door.

When a hint of watery light leaked through, she knew it was day. When the slice of space between the floor and the bottom of the door was as pitch black as the bathroom, it was night.

She'd brought her notepad to draw to pass the time, but in the darkness, she could do nothing but wait, worry, and drift into restless sleep, only to be awakened by another nightmare.

She practiced her sign language in the dark, her hands weaving into the now familiar shapes. *I'm scared. Please come find me.* And *I love you, I love you, I love you.*

She retold her favorite stories that Jorge had read to her—*The Giver, Hunger Games, Ender's Game*—from beginning to end, adding everything she could remember. Then she made up new stories and acted them out until her fingers were sore.

Dakota wanted her to hate her foster parents, but they'd given her a gift, the gift of expression, of language.

Was it still language if no one could see it?

She clenched and unclenched her hands. Did she exist, or had she disappeared, forgotten? Left here to die inside a cramped, lonely bathroom?

She waited for her foster parents to return home, apprehension squeezing her heart tighter and tighter. They never did.

Had they been in a car accident? Did the brilliant flash blind them? Had a building collapsed on them as they tried to flee from the shockwave?

Or had the bomb itself incinerated them into ash in an instant?

Nausea roiled through her empty, cramping stomach. She pressed her fist to her mouth, choking back another sob.

With every passing hour (or what she thought was an hour) her hope in her foster parents dwindled.

But still, she waited for her sister to come for her.

When she was thirsty, she drank from the sink. She'd filled it up and pushed down the stopper just in case the water stopped working. With the power out, the water would stop, too, once it got through the pipes.

Fumbling for the faucet with one hand so she wouldn't bump her head, she bent and scooped water into her mouth with the other.

Her stomach gnawed with hunger, but there was nothing she could do about that.

Time passed. The crack beneath the door turned dark, then light, then dark, and finally light again, and still Dakota wasn't here.

Why wasn't she here? Hours and hours had passed. Where could she possibly be? Didn't she know Eden was trapped here, scared and desperate and alone?

Eden blinked back tears of helpless frustration. But that just made her feel guilty. She had no right to feel anger at her sister.

Dakota wouldn't abandon her. She knew that. Dakota had promised.

And out of everyone in the whole world, only Dakota had never failed her.

It was Dakota who had saved her, again and again. Dakota who swore to never leave her. *Never, ever.*

They were sisters.

And that meant everything.

32

DAKOTA

"We want to go with you," Shay repeated.

Julio stood behind her, his hands stuffed into his pockets, looking decidedly less sure.

"There's still fallout," Dakota warned. "It's dangerous."

Dakota, Logan, Shay, and Julio stood in the empty foyer of the theater. Dim light streamed through the broken windows, highlighting the grains of fallout that had drifted inside the entrance like a deadly tide.

"There isn't enough food and water for everyone." Shay chewed on her ragged thumbnail. "If all four of us leave, they can make it."

"I'm not leaving my wife to fend for herself a second longer," Julio said, his expression resolute. "You aren't the only one with family out there."

Dakota couldn't stop them from coming. Besides, the saying was true. There was safety in numbers. Shay had some medical knowledge which might come in handy out there.

And Shay was right; the others left behind in the theater would last several days longer with four fewer people.

Dakota thought of tough Zamira, her fragile granddaughter Isabel, and little motherless Piper. Zamira had promised Dakota she'd watch over Piper and help her find surviving family members after this was all over.

They deserved to live. Dakota wanted them to live.

"All right," she said. "You're adults. You're capable of making your own decisions. If you want to come with us, I won't stop you."

"What's the plan?" Julio asked.

"First, we're rescuing my little sister. She's a bit over two miles northwest, in a suburb between Wynwood and Allapattah called Palm Cove. I don't think it'll be more than a couple of hours out of our way, but every second counts."

She ran her tongue over her bottom lip. "You need to know that you'll get more exposure than you would if you just went directly west from here to escape the fallout."

"And after you get your sister?" Shay asked, popping another piece of gum into her mouth. "What's next?"

"We're heading straight west to US 41."

"The Tamiami Trail," Julio said.

"Right." US 41 was the main route connecting east and west Florida below Lake Okeechobee. "It's around seventy-five miles from the outskirts of Miami to the outskirts of Naples. We can't take I-95, because it cuts too close to the hot zone."

She closed her eyes for a moment, imagining the complex layout of Miami in her mind's eye. "We could go west past the airport and then take the Palmetto Expressway north to I-75, then the Sawgrass Expressway. But everyone will be fleeing that way, and it bottlenecks between the Glades and the Atlantic, making things even worse.

"People are instinctive. They'll go north or south. Fewer people will go through the Glades toward Naples. It looks like it'll take longer, but it's less likely to become a parking lot, and it's free of radiation."

"A win-win, then," Logan said.

She shrugged. "It's the least worst option out of a dozen terrible options. You're welcome to head out on your own."

Shay and Julio exchanged a look.

"My aunt lives in Naples," Shay said. "My mom's on a work trip in Tallahassee, thank goodness. She'll be okay until I can get to her. So that works for me."

Julio shook his head, his eyes dark with worry. "My wife, Yoselyn, is in West Palm Beach visiting her sister. I'll stay with you until Miami International, then I'll head north."

"Fantastic," Logan said flatly.

He watched her, a hard alertness in his eyes, like he was waiting for her to bring up the safehouse.

That wasn't going to happen. She didn't trust any of them, not even Julio.

They'd keep each other alive until the Tamiami Trail. That was it. Then she'd lose all of them. She and Eden were better off on their own.

"We're all on the same page," Logan said. "Let's get this show on the road."

Shay wrapped her arms around herself and shivered despite the heat. "It's safe out there, right?"

"Nowhere is safe," Dakota said.

The world had never been safe, not for people like Dakota. Shay—with her fancy college education, cute clothes, and soft life—had no idea what the real world was like. Not then, not now.

She pushed down a flush of anger and resentment. She didn't like being that person—jealous and petty.

Dakota moved to the shattered doorway of the movie theater and pointed at the Old Navy a few storefronts away, holding the roll of duct tape Shay had rescued from the employee supply room earlier that morning.

"We need to cover ourselves from head to foot with clothes," she said. "That will help some. It won't protect us from the gamma rays, but from the beta and alpha particles at least."

She did a quick calculation in her head. "We could have been exposed to half a gray over the last forty-eight hours inside the theater. Acute radiation syndrome sets in between one and two gray. There's still some fallout in the air. Maybe five rem an hour. Maybe more."

"Which means we have to get out of the fallout zone by tonight," Logan said.

"We can do that," Shay said brightly. "I power-walk every morning for exercise. I can do four miles in an hour. Should be easy."

"Easy isn't the word for it." Dakota hesitated in the jagged doorway, dread coiling in her gut.

Over two miles of destroyed city stood between her and Eden.

What terrors awaited them out there? Would she be up to the task?

She had to be. She had no choice.

Logan strode past her. "Let's get this show on the road then, shall we?" He tapped his wrist. "Don't forget to start that timer of yours."

Dakota looked at her watch. 12:40 p.m.

Forty-eight hours ago, the first bomb in D.C. detonated. How much unimaginable suffering had millions of people endured in the seconds, minutes, and hours since?

She pushed the thought from her mind. They needed to find Eden before nightfall. Sundown was around 8:15 p.m. Less than eight hours, but they had to be out of the hot zone long before then. There wasn't a second to waste.

She stepped out into the daylight. Humidity blasted them like every other day in South Florida. Instantly, sweat beaded her forehead and lower lip and congealed beneath her pits.

The clouds were thick and dark as wounds. Tiny particles like grains of sand or salt covered everything. But no fallout fell from the sky.

At least, none that they could see.

An eerie silence wrapped around them like a thick, woolen blanket. No car engines or alarms, honking horns, or people. No birdsong, even.

Nothing but the rapid flutter of her own heartbeat in her ears. Everything was dulled, like the morning after a fresh snow.

She'd seen snow once on a road trip to southwest Michigan with her real parents when she was young—maybe five or six.

She remembered snowball fights and snow angels, scarves and mittens, the feeling of the cold eating her nose and fingers, needing to pee but being too bundled up in her snowsuit to make it.

She remembered her father's booming laughter and her mother's smiling, cold-reddened face.

But that time was dead and gone.

Dakota shoved down the memory.

Now, the only things that mattered were survival and saving Eden.

33
MADDOX

Maddox Cage believed in hell. He hadn't known quite what that hell would look like until today.

Smoke shivered, gusting, thick as fog. Ash and fine, sand-like grains fell swirling from the darkened sky like poisonous snow, sheeting everything in gray. The air smelled sulfuric, poisoned.

Blackened skeletons of fire-rotted cars scattered across the crumbled, buckled asphalt. Palm trees not already toppled were sheered of their fronds, jutting trunks blackened with char.

The further into the heart of downtown he staggered, the worse the devastation.

Everything around him had been torn from its moorings and flung apart. Buildings were unrecognizable, their roofs caved in, their insides gutted, collapsed structures with exposed skeletons of metal and beams.

His shoes crunched over piles of debris—bits of metal, rocks, and glass, chunks of twisted, deformed plastic, charred wood, and concrete ground to powder.

He couldn't walk a straight line but was forced to climb over small mountains of rubble, zigzagged past hunks of twisted, melted hulks of metal the size of houses.

He passed bodies—not people, bodies. So many bodies. Hundreds. Maybe thousands.

Bodies broken and crushed and charred. Bodies covered in ash and soot, missing legs or arms, pulverized beneath fallen ceilings and walls and cars.

Some were vaporized instantly, leaving only shadowy stains on the walls.

Some were charred where they stood, like coal statues. Others were burnt and ravaged beyond recognition—no longer human.

A man and a woman in their fifties writhed and groaned on the sidewalk outside a boutique purse shop, their torsos, necks, and faces stippled with dozens of shards of glass—they'd been standing at the window during the blast.

One figure—man or woman, he couldn't tell—limped ahead of him, its leg below the knee crushed and shattered.

Gratitude filled him. He was bruised but hale and whole. He still had his limbs. He could walk out of this carnage on his own two legs.

God had blessed him. He recognized that much.

Survivors lurched past him, almost inhuman creatures, deformed by burns, punctured by spears of glass or javelins of metal. First a few, then a dozen, then a regular stream of them.

There, a few dozen yards up the street, the blue sign for Miami North Medical Center appeared out of the haze of ash and smoke.

The street was crammed full of hundreds of bodies, all clamoring for help, for healing, for salvation that wasn't coming.

He could barely make out the building itself—damaged but still standing—for the crowd surging around it, filling the parking lot, spilling through the broken doors and windows.

It had already been overrun.

He saw no lights anywhere. For whatever reason, their generator was out. What could they possibly do for those patients they could reach without power?

The hospital could save no one, he realized dimly. Not him, not anyone. Salvation resided elsewhere.

A church rose on the left, looming above him. It was an old Catholic cathedral, the stone walls upright but listing, the roof mostly intact but for the caved-in steeple.

His gaze came to rest on a charred, life-sized statue of St. Peter. The shockwave had knocked it clear out of the sagging building. Now it lay at the bottom of the cracked stone stairs.

Vindication swelled in his chest. It served them right for worshipping graven images.

He looked at the desolation, at the fractured, ruined city.

God had done this.

What else could this be but God's wrath, descending upon the country for its sins, its worldliness?

His father had always warned him that God would destroy the polluted cities just as He'd once destroyed Sodom and Gomorrah.

That the appointed time was nigh. That they must always be ready.

God would choose the Shepherds of Mercy to enact his judgment. Earthly angels handpicked to empty the bowls of wrath upon the wicked.

Maddox was not afraid. He knew what this meant, what they'd been preparing for all this time. *For the Lord shall execute judgment by fire...*

The judgment had begun.

34
DAKOTA

Dakota led their small band along the road parallel to the storefronts, careful not to slip on the slick fallout particles or trip on debris. Glass shards littered the asphalt; even the car windows were all shattered.

Julio gestured at a brand-new Ford F-150 taking up two parking spaces. "You sure none of these will work? Our trip would be a heck of a lot faster with wheels."

He pointed to a sleek, burnt-orange sports car. "Or better yet, how about this beauty? A 2012 Mazda RX-8. I'm sure her owner won't mind if we borrow it."

"The EMP rendered everything within three miles useless," Dakota said. "Once we get out of the hot zone, we can try to find something to drive."

Julio studied the vehicles as they passed by. "If we can find an old model without any computerized gizmos, I can hotwire one."

"Really?" Logan asked, impressed.

Julio blushed. He ran a hand through his graying hair. "I spent a few summers hanging with a rough crowd as a kid. And I like cars. Especially the classics. Give me a 1961 Jaguar E-

Type or a 1969 Ferrari Dino 246 GT and I can die a happy man.

"I wanted to be a mechanic once. I like to rebuild the engines and tool around. I can fix most mechanical issues myself, could since I was thirteen. But the old man needed help with the Beer Shack. The rest is history, you know?"

"What about bikes?" Shay asked eagerly. "We could travel so much faster."

Dakota gestured at the asphalt. "There's glass and debris everywhere. You can barely see the ground. We're more likely to fall and crack our heads open five minutes in than to get where we need to go. It's too dangerous. For now."

Shay popped her gum. "Walking it is, then. At least we'll get some exercise, right?"

"That's one way to look at it," Dakota said archly.

Julio crossed himself. "The sooner we get out of here, the better."

"I didn't know you were Catholic," Logan said.

He shrugged. "Lapsed. But I guess it all comes back when the crap really hits the fan."

Dakota gave him a sharp look. "How could God allow this?"

"I don't have those answers." Julio touched the gold cross he wore around his neck as he walked. "But I know God didn't cause this evil."

"How do you know that?"

"Because God is love," Julio said simply. "We must have faith, now more than ever."

"Faith? After this? What about the hundreds of thousands of people who had faith God would keep them safe? What good is their faith now?"

"Death is not the end for them," Julio said slowly. "They'll be in heaven."

Dakota snorted. "I'd rather have my life, if it's all the same to God."

"Dakota," Shay chided gently. "I don't know about God, but this sure isn't Julio's fault. Shouldn't we respect other people's faith, even if it isn't our own?"

"We've all got to believe in something," Julio said, "especially at a time like this."

"No, we really don't." She'd had enough of religion to last several lifetimes. She believed God existed, but the only God she'd known was a God of wrath and vengeance.

The only faith she had left was in herself.

"I have faith in something." Logan veered left toward a Walgreens sandwiched between a Party City and a Chinese take-out place. "I'll catch up."

"Where are you going?" Dakota asked. "We need to find protective clothing ASAP."

"I'm...worshiping." Logan waved a hand without turning around. "Need something holy to drink."

Dakota's gut tightened. Her first foster mother had been a drunk. She'd hated the stink of it on her breath, the glassy cruelty in her eyes when she came after one of the other, more vulnerable kids.

Dakota had stepped in, given the woman a black eye for her troubles.

That foster placement hadn't lasted long.

She cursed under her breath. Did she make the right choice to bring Logan along?

Maybe she should've tried harder to steal the gun from him. She should've just set out on her own with a plan to find the closest gun shop and confiscate a new XD9 with a fine leather holster for herself.

A man with a gun was dangerous to his own group if he was a

drunk or otherwise unreliable. Even though she worked in a bar, Dakota never drank.

She hated the thought of losing control for even a minute.

She wouldn't have chosen the Beer Shack if she'd had a choice, but Julio was the only boss willing to overlook her paranoid idiosyncrasies and pay her under the table.

"We're not waiting for him," she snapped at Julio and Shay, who had both stopped. "Let's go."

They picked their way across the parking lot and entered the store, careful to avoid the jagged chunks of glass still embedded in the metal frames of the front doors. The interior was deeply shadowed. Dakota pulled her flashlight out of her pocket and flicked it on.

Near the front, all the racks of clothing had been knocked over. The huge display sign hanging from the ceiling had fallen and fractured, huge chunks of plastic scattered across the floor.

A dozen mannequins littered the glossy cement floor, some without arms, legs, or heads, but dressed in bright screen T-shirts and acid-washed skinny jeans.

Further inside, the white checkout counter gleamed dimly, surrounded by dark hulking racks that loomed out of the shadows like crouching monsters, predators just waiting to attack.

"Hey, Dakota." Shay stood before a rack of striped long-sleeved shirts, her arms crossed over her chest, chewing her lower lip nervously. "Should we touch these? Haven't they been exposed to radiation?"

"Yeah, they have. Check the back storeroom for clothes still sealed in boxes," Dakota said as she moved toward the checkout counter. "They'll be the safest."

"Looks cozy in here." Logan came up beside her, so quietly she'd hardly noticed. He clutched a bottle of gin by the neck. It was half-empty. "It was the only one I could find that wasn't broken. Such a pity."

"Did you already drink all that?"

He took a long swallow and wiped the back of his mouth. "Isn't that what it's for? What better time to drown your sorrows than the apocalypse?"

"I can't think of a worse time. You need your wits about you."

He glanced down at her, his eyes already a bit shiny, but there was an alertness there, too. "Something you're extra worried about?"

She tensed. She didn't like how he was looking at her, like he could see the secrets she held tight inside herself.

She wasn't telling him a thing. Not about her past, not about Maddox—not unless she had to. She didn't trust him as far as she could throw him.

Right now, she wished she'd left them all behind.

35
DAKOTA

"As if all this isn't enough?" Dakota stared at Logan, daring him to challenge her further.

Logan met her gaze for another moment, his jaw working like he wanted to say something else, like maybe he suspected she had an ulterior motive.

He dropped his eyes first. Logan gave a careless shrug and took another swig. "The world's been a dumpster fire for a long time."

"So, you should know better."

His mouth tightened. "I know to take pleasure where you can find it. And I don't take orders from anyone—least of all you."

Irritation flared through her. "You're in this group, you answer to me."

He let out a sharp bark of laughter. "You think you're the leader?"

"We sure as hell aren't following a drunken idiot," she shot back.

"Guys, let's just take a breath." Julio stepped between them, hands out. She could just make out his tense, pleading expression in the glow of the flashlight. "We're on the same side here, right? Time is the enemy, not each other."

He was right. Damn it.

Logan gestured with the gin bottle. "Fine by me."

"Fine," she grumbled.

"Here." With his free hand, Logan pulled his Glock 43 from beneath his shirt. He kept it angled down but held it out. "Happy now?"

"You have a *gun?*" Shay squeaked. She took a step away, bumping into a sunglasses stand, lifting her palms, as if Logan had just brandished a live grenade.

"Sure looks like it," Logan said.

Her eyes went wide. "All this time—in the theater, with kids around—you had a gun?"

"He already answered the question," Dakota snapped.

"Guns are dangerous! What if a kid had gotten ahold of it? Or it discharged accidentally? Someone could've gotten hurt!"

"Hold on a minute." Logan took another swig of gin. "I know what I'm doing. A gun is a tool, just like anything else. It's not a bomb waiting to go off."

Julio flinched.

Logan only gave an indifferent shrug.

"I'm not trying to cause a fight or anything, but..." Shay pursed her lips, staring at them reproachfully. "But you hid it like—like a criminal!" Her voice rose. "You should've told us you had it!"

"Frankly, it's none of your damn business."

Shay opened her mouth, not saying anything for a second as her outrage warred with her desire to be pleasant and polite. "Well—I—I'm just trying to understand what would possess you—"

"This is a waste of time," Dakota broke in. "Like I said before, you're welcome to leave at any time. No one's twisting your arm here."

Shay gnawed on her thumbnail, her anxious gaze jumping from Dakota to Logan. She took a slow, steadying breath. "I'm—I'm sorry. I'm not trying to cause drama. I just—I really hate guns."

Logan stared at her like she was from another planet.

"You're entitled to your opinion, and we're entitled to ours. The gun stays. No discussion." Dakota clenched her jaw and stalked past them.

Shay and Julio straggled along silently behind her, Shay appropriately chagrined enough to keep her mouth shut.

Logan remained near the front of the store, rifling through a fallen rack of women's plaid long-sleeved shirts with the muzzle of the gun. With his free hand, he knocked back more gin.

She gritted her teeth in frustration. They weren't cut out for this. She definitely should've left Shay and Julio behind.

And Logan, too, for that matter.

They were dead weight. They were too pampered; they couldn't understand the reality of their brave new world.

Dakota didn't have the time or the patience to explain it to them. She'd thought Logan was someone who got it, but he was acting like a drunken idiot.

She had half a mind to tell him to forget the whole thing right now. He was more trouble than it was worth.

She could defend herself just fine, as long as she had a decent pistol and plenty of ammo. How hard could it be to find a gun?

If worse came to worse, there were people who'd been carrying who'd died from their injuries. Their bodies would still be out there, ripe for the scavenging.

The thought sent a shudder of revulsion through her, but she was nothing if not practical.

They were dead. They were in Heaven or Hell or Nirvana or Valhalla, depending on what they believed.

At any rate, they didn't care about their guns anymore. If it were her, she'd want someone living to find some use out of the weapons that had served her well.

She adjusted the plan in her mind. Maybe she could lose Logan right now—

Boom!

The crack splintered the air. Small chunks of concrete sprayed a foot in front of the clothing rack directly in front of her.

The gunshot rang in her ears. Her heart exploded against her ribs.

Instinctively, Dakota dropped to the floor, already fumbling for her knife with her free hand.

"Don't you move," came a low, hard voice from deep in the shadowed store, "or I'll blow your head clean off."

36
LOGAN

Logan spun and dove behind the toppled clothing rack, his pulse thudding against his throat. The clothes offered zero protection from a bullet, but maybe the hostile hadn't seen him yet.

If not, he still had the advantage of stealth and surprise.

Damn it straight to hell. He should've cleared the damn store before they'd even stepped foot inside. He'd allowed himself to be distracted by the booze and the waitress.

He knew better.

Human nature was human nature, regardless of what atrocities surrounded them.

Looting always came with chaos. Always. Someone had been smart enough to seize an opportunity where he saw it.

"We're not here to hurt anyone," Julio stammered, his hands lifted high in the air. "We just need a few things."

"You and everyone else," the voice responded. "Ain't no-one takin' what belongs to us."

Logan peered around the corner of the rack, trying to make out the figure but he was still too deeply swathed in shadow. From his voice, Logan guessed male, Hispanic, youngish. Maybe early to mid-twenties. Probably a gangbanger.

"Are you the storeowner?" Julio asked, still attempting diplomacy. "We can pay for what we need."

"Screw that." The guy gave a hard laugh. "We took over ownership. No one here to say otherwise. Imagine that."

"We're not armed," Dakota said. "You can put that gun down."

"Liars *and* thieves, then. Drop the knife you got there unless you want a hole drilled into your skull."

Dakota's knife clattered to the floor.

"Do you see any other weapons?" Dakota said. "We aren't a threat to you."

"We're people trying to survive the bomb, just like you," Julio said calmly.

"From where I'm standing, you people are the ones breakin' and enterin'. That makes you the criminals in this scenario."

"We didn't know anyone was here," Shay stammered.

Hunched low behind the clothes, Logan quietly set the liquor bottle on the cement floor and gripped the gun with both hands. His vision blurred a bit as the familiar warm buzz enveloped him.

His thoughts came stiff and jerky. He shook his head hard to clear his mind.

Think. He had to act without doubt or hesitation.

Their lives depended on it.

"We'll just leave, then." Shay's voice shook. "No worries. We'll go somewhere else. We're sorry for bothering you."

"Now see, there ain't nowhere else to go. We're taking care of things."

If he could circle around the far side of the checkout counter, using the clothing racks as cover, he could flank the hostile and take a clear shot.

The next closest rack was about five feet away. It was tall, displaying colorful maxi dresses with a connecting T-shaped shorter rack of cropped jean jackets.

He could make it.

He stifled his breathing, his pulse loud in his ears, and pushed into a crouch, gun at the low ready, finger nestled against the trigger guard.

He darted between the racks and paused again, assessing. One more rack—this one of button-up blouses—and he'd be even with the counter.

"What do you mean?" Dakota asked. "Who's we?"

She was stalling. Smart girl.

"Blood Outlaws. Chapter of the Latin Kings. Thousands strong and growing by the day. Maybe you ain't heard of us in your fancy digs, but you sure know us now. We're taking over the city."

"The city is burning," Dakota said.

"Not most of it. Not here. We're here to make sure everythin' still standin' stays that way."

"The police—" Shay started.

"Are gone." He laughed harshly. "Dead or fled, makes no difference. When the smoke clears, we'll be the ones in control. And we'll do a better job of running this city, too."

Moving in a crouch, Logan dashed to the next rack. Several sleeves fluttered from his movement.

He held his breath and waited.

The hostile started to turn.

"What about the fallout?" Dakota said quickly. "There's still radiation everywhere—"

"Man, that's just the government lyin' to us to keep us scared and out of the city. They don't know nothin'. Ain't nothing falling from the sky."

Logan peeked around the side of the rack. The light from the storefront windows shone dim and grimy.

The beam of Dakota's flashlight was angled up at the ceiling, but Logan could still make out the scene before him.

Five yards to his left, the hostile leaned against the white counter next to one of the cash registers.

He was a short and skinny Latino in his late teens, dressed in saggy, oversized shorts and a gray wife-beater tank top. Gang and prison tattoos sleeved both of his light brown arms. Greasy black hair stuck to his scalp and neck.

He gripped an M4 carbine low, with one hand, like Rambo in the movies—which meant he wasn't well-trained and didn't know the force of his own weapon.

But Dakota and the others stood only fifteen feet away from him. The punk could still easily kill all three of them with a wild spray of gunfire.

"If I just let thieves go free, this fine city'll descend into anarchy," he continued. "Can't let that happen."

"I agree," Julio said amiably. "Crime's been a problem here for a while. And now without the police? It'll be even worse. You're a good man for willingly stepping into the gap."

The thug sniffed. "Damn right. The Blood Outlaws make the rules now. We're the ones gonna keep everythin' going, you feel me?"

Logan watched as Dakota and Julio exchanged tense glances.

"We aren't thieves," Dakota said. "We didn't take anything."

"You've gotta pay a contribution toward the cause. It ain't easy protecting this city from the criminal element."

"We don't have any—" Shay started.

Julio held up his hand, silencing her. "I'm sure you're doing everything you can. It takes a lot to protect a city."

Blood Outlaw nodded along with him, his knee juddering. "We're working hard to restore order, here!"

"And we appreciate it," Julio spoke in a placid, reassuring tone. "The fine citizens of Miami appreciate it."

He just rolled his eyes. "Whatever, man."

Julio was trying hard to talk him down by agreeing with him, sympathizing with his plight, no matter how far-fetched, the same way Logan had seen him do with aggressive drunks at the Beer Shack a hundred times.

But the thug was too keyed up.

"Empty your pockets," he demanded with a thick, phlegmy cough. "Take that ring off. Yeah, I see it. Toss it on the counter."

"Please," Julio said, the first hint of fear entering his voice. "It's my wedding ring. We've been married twenty-six years. It's not worth much—"

"It's gold; it's worth somethin'. We've already hit every jewelry store in the city. We're rolling in gold and diamonds. Gold's the currency of the future." Blood Outlaw waved the carbine at them. "Gold, pills, and bullets."

"I have cash," Dakota said quickly. "Let him keep the ring. I'll give you five hundred bucks."

"Cash ain't good for nothin' anymore. That advice, I'm givin' to you for free. Take off the ring. Now."

Julio rubbed his ring, hesitating.

"Just do it," Dakota said.

For a second, she glanced over Blood Outlaw's shoulder.

Logan knew she could see him there, hidden in the shadows behind the rack, but her gaze never landed on him. Her eyes gave nothing away. "Whatever he says, do it."

"It's just a thing," Shay whispered. "It's not her. It's okay."

Julio nodded and held up the ring. "I've got it right here. I'll pay the tax. Take this in appreciation for everything you've done."

Blood Outlaw scowled at him suspiciously, suspecting a trick.

Logan watched Julio step forward and place his wedding band gently on the counter. The Blood Outlaw snatched it up with his free hand and jammed it in his pocket.

Anger mingled with the buzzing in Logan's blood.

In all the months he'd frequented the Beer Shack, Julio had been nothing but kind and polite. He always talked about his wife with fondness—one of the rare truly happily married.

Julio's wife might already be dead. Even if she were alive, Julio had lost his livelihood, his home, probably most of his friends, his city.

He didn't deserve to lose his wedding band, too.

It was wrong. And it pissed Logan off.

He'd known plenty of pissants like this guy in the old days. Just puffed up gangster wannabes.

The thug acted like he ruled the roost, but he was just a grunt assigned to keep an eye on a pathetic strip mall. Just a throwaway, a disposable foot soldier.

And not a very good one. He was arrogant and cocky. He didn't respect the weapon he was waving around, hadn't even bothered to learn the right stance, the correct grip.

And there was something wrong with him—in his sickly pallor, in the sluggish way he moved.

Logan just needed a moment. A second of inattention, an instant for the muzzle of that M4 to point away from the group.

Just one.

37
LOGAN

They're not your responsibility. That voice, whispering inside Logan's head again.

It'd be far easier to wait for whatever was going to happen to happen, then walk away with his booze and forget about this whole thing.

Maybe find a nice, cozy, empty mansion and curl up and die a slow death from radiation poisoning. Or he could set out alone, journey north and find his own way out of this mayhem.

He wasn't even sure why he'd said yes to the waitress. He was better off on his own. It was safer for everyone; hadn't he learned that the hard way?

But he already loathed this Blood Outlaw and everything he stood for. Preying on the weak when the city—the whole country—was on its knees.

Whenever anyone asked, Logan always insisted he didn't believe in morals, in right and wrong.

He was lying.

As if Dakota could read his thoughts, she slowly tilted her

raised hand until the flashlight beam no longer pointed at the ceiling, but a few yards to the right of the counter.

It lit up the area so clearly that Logan could see the gangster's finger twitching on the trigger. The guy half-turned for a moment, coughing, and spat a sour-smelling liquid onto the floor.

Logan caught a glimpse of his profile: gaunt face, a pallid, yellowish tinge to his skin.

The thug had radiation sickness.

He was a dead man walking.

"We gave you what you asked for," Shay said. "Can we please just go now?"

Blood Outlaw chuckled darkly. "Listen to this one. Damn girl, you're funny. And fine. What're you doin' with these gringos? Come with me, and I'll have you set up in a nice-ass mansion in Bay Point with an ocean view by tonight."

Shay flinched. Her hands were still in the air, but she shrank in on herself. Gone were the cheery smile and bright eyes. She looked terrified.

In contrast, Dakota didn't look so much frightened as furious. But her voice was deadly calm as she spoke. "We've given you what we've got. We're not a threat. We're leaving."

"I know you don't want to hurt anyone," Julio added, still trying to placate the guy. "You're a good guy, just doing what you have to. We've made our contribution. No reason to wear out our welcome."

Blood Outlaw snorted. "I've gotta worry about me and mine now. Nobody else matters. You could go tell somebody what I got here. Or maybe I let you go, and you sneak around back and try and take us by surprise, steal from the brotherhood."

He coughed and wiped his mouth, swaying a bit on his feet. "Or maybe you got uglier ideas in those fine li'l heads."

He smiled lazily, half-turning, and swung the M4 in a slow

arc, pointing first at Shay, then Julio, then Dakota. "I could sit here and kill each one of you, like target practice. Pow, pow, pow."

Sweat trickled down his temple. Circles of sweat drenched the neck of his tank top and ringed his armpits. "Right? You feel me? There ain't nobody to stop us now. No cops. No politicians. We're the kings now. We make the rules. *I* make the rules."

Logan shifted into a kneeling position, one knee up, and rested his elbows on his thighs to steady his arms. The booze made his head swim, but he forced himself to focus, sighting the back of the gangster's head.

There were easier targets—his shoulder, his long, skinny back—but anything other than a kill shot would allow the thug to pull the trigger.

Blood Outlaw jerked his chin at Shay. "Come here, girl."

Shay whimpered.

He wiped his mouth with the back of his hand and spat. He swayed again, then straightened. Sweat dripped down the sides of his face.

"Maybe I'll let y'all go out of the goodness of my heart," he drawled, grinning. "But maybe we'll have a little fun first. Just a kiss, girl, for payment. It's a dangerous world out there without us to protect you."

Shay didn't move.

"Look, I know you're a decent guy," Julio said. "A real man. You don't want to hurt a lady—"

"Shut up!" Blood Outlaw aimed the M4 at Shay. "I said, come here!"

Shay took an obedient step closer.

"Don't," Dakota said sharply.

Come on, come on. Logan just needed the guy to wave the carbine one more time, to angle it away from them.

Adrenaline shot through his veins. His senses sharpened.

That familiar sense of power surged through him: life and death balanced in his hands. It was intoxicating, exhilarating.

Except his hands were trembling, ever so slightly.

The thrill was still there, that pulsing energy lighting up his synapses. But so was the dread, a screw turning tighter and tighter in his gut.

Sweat dripped down Logan's forehead. His nerves were jangling, a buzzing in his blood.

You can't take the shot, a voice whispered in his booze-soaked brain.

An image flashed through his mind—a child crying, a woman on her knees, begging, *no, no, no, no*...the gunshot blast, reverberating up his arm.

The tiny body falling, endlessly falling.

He blinked furiously, willing away the images, the nightmares. He had to focus, to think clearly.

This guy was a scumbag like all the others. How many had he beaten or shot? How many had he killed without guilt or conscience? A dozen? Two dozen?

None since that night.

The truth was, he enjoyed it. He'd derived pleasure and power from violence, right up until the end. That pleasure was tempting him again, thrumming through him in tandem with his heartbeat.

But the darkness was there, too. A swirling mass of nothingness sucking him in, beckoning to him.

If he fell, he'd never come back.

Dakota slowly lowered her hands, but kept the thug in the light. "We're leaving now, and you're not going to stop us."

Julio gestured for Shay. "Come on, let's go."

Shay stood there, trembling, scared and indecisive.

"You better move," Outlaw growled, taking an aggressive step toward them. He wavered a moment, then regained his footing, his grimace twisting into a sneer. He flailed the M4 to make his point.

That was Logan's chance.

Maybe the only one he was going to get.

Logan pushed out the darkness, the self-loathing, the blur of the booze, and the anticipation he couldn't quite kill buzzing in the back of his brain.

The carbine swung in slow motion, arcing toward Dakota.

Logan steadied his hands and inched out from the right side of the rack, his aim straight and true, the sight tracking the center of the gangbanger's skull.

At the last instant, he angled his aim slightly down.

Shay caught his movement.

Her terrified gaze slid from Blood Outlaw's carbine to Logan behind him.

Blood Outlaw saw it. "What the hell—"

He whirled, half-staggering, the carbine twisting with him, his finger pressing down on the trigger.

Logan took the shot.

38
LOGAN

Shay screamed.

The thug's body spun sideways from the force of the shot striking his right shoulder. He slumped against the counter with a pained grunt.

The M4 let loose a spray of bullets as it swung, most of the shots hitting the walls and ceiling above the group's head as they arced across the open space and shattered the heads of a family of mannequins displayed next to the fitting rooms.

The gunshots ringing in his ears, Logan was on his feet in an instant, dodging the clothing rack and charging the counter. He put another bullet in the man's right arm above the bicep.

Blood Outlaw shrieked and fumbled for the carbine, blood spurting from the wound in his shoulder.

Logan reached him in five long strides.

The thug swung at him with his uninjured arm, but Logan was faster. He ducked the high, wild blow and drove into his torso, slamming the man's spine against the counter behind them.

Blood Outlaw landed a wobbly strike to the right side of his jaw.

Logan barely felt the sting. He threw several quick, powerful jabs into the man's left kidney with his left hand.

Blood Outlaw could barely lift his arms to defend himself from the blows. His movements were sluggish, weak.

After only a few brutal seconds, he stopped fighting back.

But Logan couldn't stop hitting him. Using the butt of his Glock, he punched him in the face, the jaw, the stomach, the vulnerable shoulder.

Again and again, he hammered the man, flesh and bone giving way with wet *thwacks* beneath his rage. Blood sprayed Logan's shirt and speckled his face.

Blood Outlaw let out a slew of slurred curses as he slid down the front of the counter and sagged against the floor.

He no longer posed a threat.

Logan tucked his pistol in his waistband, bent and seized the M4, jerked the strap over the thug's head. He flipped the carbine and smashed the stock into his nose.

The man moaned. Half his face was a mashed, mangled mess. Blood spurted from his shoulder and arm, stained his tank top, and dripped onto the floor.

With stinging, trembling hands, Logan set the carbine down on the counter.

He stood over him, adrenaline pumping, breathing hard.

He resisted the urge to kick the asshole a dozen more times, to use him as a bloody punching bag until he'd purged all the terrible emotions slashing through him.

He flexed his hands, feeling the soreness, the sting, and the strength.

He could kill this man.

End his pitiful, pathetic life right now. For an instant, for a sickening, desperate moment, he wanted to.

His stomach lurched. He felt ill—and exhilarated. The

euphoria after winning a fight, after beating another man senseless with your own bare fists—it was a heady, intoxicating thing.

Almost as addictive as booze. Maybe it was more so.

Only one thing had been able to break the addiction.

That night, he'd been forced to look into Hell itself, like a mirror reflecting his own rotting heart.

He'd sworn never to go back to that life. In four years, he hadn't used his skills to engage in a single lethal fight.

He'd never crossed that line. He'd never wanted to.

Until now.

A sense of enormous power pumped through his veins. He felt more alive, more awake and invigorated than he had in years.

But the darkness had awakened within him, too.

A monster locked in a deep pit, hungry and waiting, always ready to strike.

With the darkness came the desire. For vengeance, for blood. For violence, to hurt someone else until he didn't hurt anymore.

The past never died. The darkness was always there, the monster crouching over his shoulder.

Who was he kidding, to think that a new city and a placid, uneventful life after prison would make it go away?

It waited for him. Waited for that moment when he would lose control.

Logan took a slow, deliberate step backward.

Today wasn't that day. Not yet.

He'd made a promise to himself.

He wasn't about to break it for this pissant.

He spat on the thug. "You're not special. You're a piece of trash in the garbage dump of humanity. Not even worth the energy it'd take to pull the trigger."

Blood Outlaw's head lolled back with another moan.

Something thudded in the back of the store.

"A second hostile!" Fresh adrenaline spiking through his veins, Logan spun and swung the M4 up and around.

He couldn't see past the fitting rooms situated in the middle of the store between the checkout counter and the rear of the store.

The hostile could be anywhere.

A shadow flitted across double racks of hanging clothing along the far wall.

There was no time to assess the risk or even to aim properly. He pulled the trigger. *Click.*

The M4 was empty. Utterly useless.

He dropped it and went for his pistol.

In the back, a door squealed open. Fast footsteps pounded across the floor, a metal door clanging shut. The hostile was escaping out the back exit.

Heart thudding against his ribs, he crouched low and started around the counter. "He'll alert the rest of the gang. I'll go after him—"

"Logan!" Julio's voice was strained.

He almost kept going. But something about the frantic way Julio said his name stopped him dead in his tracks. Dread sprouted in his gut as he followed Julio's gaze.

A few yards away, Shay lay sprawled across the floor.

Blood gushed from the girl's head, drenching her hair and running in rivulets down the side of her face.

It was everywhere. It puddled in her collarbone and leaked onto the concrete in oily black rings.

One of the stray bullets had found its mark.

Shay had been shot.

39

LOGAN

Logan stared down at Shay's crumpled body, at the red-black blood leaking in an ever-widening circle across the concrete floor. His Glock 43 hung limply at his side.

Heavy shadows swathed the checkout counter, the clothing racks, the toppled mannequins. Dim daylight leaked through the shattered windows at the front of the store.

Logan felt nauseous. His stomach roiled. It wasn't from the blood. He'd seen plenty before, including his own.

Shay was lying here because of him, because of what he hadn't done.

This is what happened, what always happened.

People got hurt around him. Most of the time, people that deserved it.

But there had been mistakes. Like the night four years ago that still haunted his dreams...

The darkness was in him. Even when he tried to escape it, it still managed to do harm.

"I need to stop the bleeding!" Dakota knelt beside the girl. Her hands hovered above Shay's bleeding head. "I don't want to use my bare hands...Julio, grab shopping bags. They should be somewhere behind the checkout counter—in a cupboard if you can—less contamination that way."

Julio hurriedly brought over a handful of plastic bags. "What else?"

Dakota slipped one over each hand. "I need shirts! The flannel ones!"

Julio scrambled to obey. He dashed around the counter and ran toward the back of Old Navy.

Dakota set the flashlight beside her and frantically searched Shay's bloodied skull for the head wound. The beam limned the frantic scene in shades of black and white.

In the harsh shadows, all Logan could make out was Shay's matted, tightly coiled curls and more blood. Blood splotched Shay's face and stained Dakota's fingers.

Shay's eyes were closed.

She lay still. Too still.

Julio brought a handful of shirts and flannel sweaters and sank down beside them. "I—I grabbed them from some boxes in the storeroom. They were sealed in plastic, so they're free of contamination."

Dakota grabbed a shirt and tried to soak up the blood. It just kept coming. "Help me!"

Julio reared back on his heels, swaying a little. He looked ready to pass out. "I'm sorry—I'm not good with blood..."

Dakota swore. "Move aside!"

Logan pulled Julio to his feet and steadied him. "You okay?"

"Yeah, fine." Julio sagged against the counter. He scraped his hands nervously through his graying black hair. His bronze skin was ashen. "Thanks, man."

"Julio, take the flashlight. I need to see!" Dakota said. "Logan, I need your help to stop this blood!"

Logan turned back toward the rear exit. "What about the second hostile? I should go—"

"It's too late." Dakota gave a sharp shake of her head. "If he's going for his superiors, I bet they're smart enough to stay out of the hot zone. Which means he won't be returning any time soon."

Logan longed to go after him, but she was right.

A good forty-five seconds had already passed.

The second guy had fled. He could've turned down an alley, sought refuge in any of the businesses lining the street, disappeared into the same rat hole he'd come from.

The gangbanger was long gone.

Another error.

He was rusty. Too slow to react, to act swiftly and decisively, his senses dulled by the booze. He used to be sharp and deadly as a honed blade. Used to be.

Uneasiness lurched in Logan's gut. He had the feeling they'd end up regretting that mistake—and badly.

It would cost them. He just didn't know how much yet.

"I hope you're right," he said stiffly.

"Logan!" Dakota jerked her chin at him. "Come on! Help me staunch the blood!"

He crouched on the other side of Shay and set the M4 close beside him, the handgun next to it within easy reach. He remained on his feet, just in case.

He turned so he was perpendicular to both the front and rear of the store, keeping an alert eye on both exits. Twenty feet in front of him, Blood Outlaw slumped, unconscious.

Nothing and no one would take him by surprise again.

He slipped a plastic bag over each hand and pressed the cloth to Shay's head. "Will she make it?" he asked grimly.

Dakota spared him a single searing glance. "How should I know?"

Julio aimed the flashlight at Shay's head with one hand, his other clenched around the gold cross at his neck. His mouth moved in a silent prayer.

Logan didn't pray. He didn't know how. In that moment, he desperately wanted to believe in something, a higher power, hope, a miracle.

Instead, shame and dread and horror opened up beneath him like a gaping maw.

This is your fault, that voice whispered in his head. *It's who you are. The sooner you face it, the better for everyone else.*

He shoved that thought down deep. There wasn't time to stew in guilt and self-pity now.

He focused on the girl, every fiber of his being willing her to open her damn eyes.

40

DAKOTA

Dark liquid seeped into Dakota's pants at the knees. The puddle beneath Shay's head widened, gleaming blackly in the flashlight beam.

There was so much blood. It didn't seem possible that so much could be contained within a single human body.

But it could. She knew that well enough. An image flitted through her mind—the dead body at her feet, blood spilling everywhere.

She should just run. Part of her wanted to get the hell out of here and forget these people.

She wasn't responsible for them. She didn't owe them anything.

Her sister was the one who needed her.

Guilt tugged at her. What was she going to do? Just leave Shay bleeding on the ground? Abandon them when they'd put their trust in her?

She couldn't do that.

Sometimes she hated that part of herself. Maybe it was a

weakness, that inability to shrug off responsibility for another human being.

It was the very thing that had kept her at the compound for so long. It would've been far easier to escape without Eden. Maybe the Shepherds wouldn't have bothered hunting for her. Eden was the one they wanted.

But Dakota had never been able to leave anyone behind.

Not Eden, and not Shay.

"We need to take her to a hospital," Julio said, distraught.

"Which one?" Dakota said tersely. "Miami North Memorial went up in flames. Aventura and North Shore are both in the hot zone, so they'll have been evacuated. The next closest hospital is, what, a four-mile walk at least? And it's been two days since the attack. They'll be overwhelmed with all the bombing victims."

"What about an emergency FEMA camp? I could go out and search for one," Julio said, touching his gold cross with one trembling hand. "Maybe there's one closer."

Dakota rolled her eyes. "Where? Which direction? We're still in the area affected by the EMP. Until we get at least three miles out, we're running blind until we find a first responder, a radio, or someone who can give us information."

"Besides, if we try to pick her up, we could cause even more damage," Logan said.

He was right. Dakota stared down at the red gradually staining the teal and brown plaid shirt in her hands and chewed anxiously on her bottom lip.

They couldn't call 911. There were no ambulances coming with screaming sirens. No hospitals or medical centers nearby with nurses and doctors waiting, a pristine, sterilized operating room at the ready.

It was up to her to save Shay.

"We've got to stop the bleeding and get her conscious," Dakota said, "then we'll reassess."

Logan and Julio nodded tightly.

The seconds passed with torturous slowness.

"Come on, come on," Dakota muttered.

"Check her pulse," Logan said, a line forming between his thick brows. "Maybe she—"

Shay groaned.

Relief flooded through Dakota's veins.

"Oh, thank God," Julio said.

Shay thrashed to life beneath their hands. More blood gushed, leaking through the layers of fabric and wetting Dakota's fingers.

Logan grabbed two clean shirts from the pile and tossed one to Dakota. "Stop moving!" he grunted to Shay.

Together, they pressed the new cloth to Shay's head. She writhed, and the shirt slipped, more blood leaking out.

"Shay!" Dakota cried. "Hold still!"

Shay moaned. Her eyelids fluttered, her eyes rolling wildly.

"Stay with us, Shay. Come on!"

She moaned again and twisted beneath Dakota and Logan's hands.

Logan dropped the shirt and gently pinned her shoulders, trying to keep her from moving. "Hold still, girl!"

Slowly, her eyes stopped rolling back in her head.

Her frenetic gaze focused on Logan's and Dakota's faces above her.

She stilled and took several shallow, rasping breaths, her wide, stunned eyes showing the whites all the way around her irises. "My head—what...happened?"

"You got shot," Logan said.

Shay's features contorted in pain—and fear.

At least she was lucid. That had to be a good sign.

"Stay with us," Dakota said. "Don't panic. You're fine. You're gonna be fine."

"We really need your medical expertise here," Julio said from a safe distance, panic in his voice. He leaned unsteadily against the checkout counter. "Tell us how to help you."

"How—how bad is it?" Shay forced out.

Dakota pushed aside a handful of Shay's thick, blood-drenched coils to see her scalp. Logan daubed the shirt quickly and lifted it even as fresh blood welled into the wound.

A long, jagged gash sliced her scalp a few inches above her right ear. Beneath the gushing blood and raw, mangled flesh, Dakota glimpsed a streak of white bone.

She let out a sharp breath. "I don't see any holes."

"How sure are you?" Julio asked.

Dakota scowled. "Do I look like a doctor to you? Not freakin' sure at all."

"A tangential...gunshot wound," Shay murmured.

Julio blanched. "That sounds bad."

"Hopefully, it didn't breach the skull...or cause...herniation of the brain."

"That sounds even worse," Julio said.

Anxiety tightened in Dakota's gut. There was far too much blood. If they couldn't stop it soon, it wouldn't matter whether the bullet pierced her brain or not.

"Mother Mary and Joseph," Julio muttered frantically. "If we don't do something, she's gonna die right here."

"No, she's not." Dakota stared straight at Shay, her hands steady, her voice even. "You're not going to die. That is not an option, do you understand? I will not let you die."

41

LOGAN

"Tell us what to do," Logan said.

Shay lifted a trembling hand and gingerly touched the side of her head. Her fingers came back dripping wet. "Head wounds—they bleed a lot. All those superficial veins and arteries beneath the skin...twenty percent of the heart's pumped blood goes to—the brain..."

Dakota threw aside a drenched shirt and grabbed a new one from the pile. "We don't need an anatomy lesson. What do we need to *do*?"

"Elevate my—feet," Shay forced out. "T-twelve inches."

Logan jerked a huge armful of soft, oversized T-shirts off a nearby rack and thrust them gently beneath Shay's feet.

Julio found a bunch of shoes to make the pile taller. Maybe the clothes and shoes were contaminated, but in the moment, it didn't matter.

Shay's walnut-brown skin took on a sickly pallor. She inhaled rapid, shallow breaths.

"What else?" Julio asked.

"C-cold. Keep me warm...to prevent shock."

"We need to cover her," Dakota said.

Logan draped a few of the flannel sweaters over Shay's arms and legs.

"How's the...bleeding?" Shay asked.

Logan lifted the shirt. Fresh blood spurted from the long, ragged gash. "Like a hose."

"Large scalp wounds with...persistent bleeding should be closed immediately...a running interlocking stitch is...most effective and will provide better hemostasis," Shay said, as if reciting from a textbook.

She grimaced. "There's no way I can do it myself...anyone here sutured a wound before?"

"I have," Dakota said.

Logan stared at Dakota in surprise. "You have?"

"Didn't I just say that?"

"You have medical experience?" Julio asked, as astonished as Logan.

"Not exactly." She looked down at Shay, her mouth pressed into a grim line. "It won't be pretty, but I can get it done."

Shay didn't even blink. "Do it."

Logan had seen more than his share of blood and guts, but sewing this girl up without anesthetic wouldn't be fun for anyone.

Still, he found himself impressed with Shay's level head and composure. He'd witnessed grown men weeping like children at lesser wounds.

That was the thing about getting shot or knifed for the first time; you never knew how someone—even yourself—would react.

He hadn't given her a second thought back in the theater, with her pretty perkiness and relentless positivity. He'd assumed she was just another gum-chewing airhead. He was beginning to realize how wrong he was.

"What do we need?" he asked her.

"If only we could order Amazon Prime...a suture kit delivered by drone...in an hour," Shay mumbled. She was trying to stay upbeat, even though she was the one who'd missed a bullet to the brain by a few millimeters.

"Save your breath for the important stuff," Dakota warned. "Needle and thread will work in a pinch, won't it?"

"Guess this qualifies...as a pinch."

"It'll leave an ugly scar."

"I know."

"Tell us what you need, damn it!" Logan interrupted. "We can get supplies from the Walgreens next door."

Shay closed her eyes briefly, took a deep breath. "Bottles of water to irrigate the wound. Gauze. Topical antibiotic. Medical tape. A sewing needle and dental floss—but not mint—that we can sterilize."

"What else?" Logan asked.

"And...scissors and a razor. You're gonna have to shave my scalp. And then suture it."

"Fantastic." Dakota gestured at Julio. "You go back to the pharmacy and get everything she just said. Logan, you stay and help me."

Julio set the flashlight on its side facing them. He turned, still swaying slightly, and jogged for the front doors.

"Bring as much booze as you can carry," Logan called after him.

"Focus, Logan," Dakota said. "Will you soak up the blood so I can see what I'm doing?"

Logan suppressed a tight smile. He didn't mind a girl ordering him around when she knew what she was doing. Dakota had proved herself plenty capable.

He grabbed a fresh shirt, balled it up, and pressed it gently to

Shay's scalp. Was the blood flow slowing? He couldn't tell through the girl's matted coils.

"You had the shot," Dakota said in a low voice.

He jerked his head up. "What?"

She stared at him accusingly, her eyes dark and glistening in the ghostly flashlight beam. "You had a kill shot and you didn't take it."

He kept underestimating this girl. He tried to hide his surprise—and his guilt. "It was dark and people were moving—"

"Bull!"

"Maybe I just wasn't good enough."

"We both know that's a load of bunk."

Her gaze traveled from the tattoos sleeving the gangbanger's arms and neck to his own. She took in the crosses, the snake and skull, the barbed wire, and the smudged, rougher markings on his hands—the five points below his thumb.

When her eyes met his again, they narrowed with suspicion. "Just what kind of soldier are you?"

He knew the time would come, sooner or later. He never should've let her believe the lie in the first place. At the time, it had seemed convenient.

Now, it made him feel like a grade-A asshole.

"I'm not," he forced out.

"What the hell are you talking about?"

"I never said I was. You made that assumption yourself."

"You didn't bother to correct me, now, did you?"

He had no answer for that one.

"Those five tattooed points on your hand. You were in prison."

He stiffened. "That's none of your business."

She flashed him a scathing look. "The hell it is. You just put us all in danger. Who are you, really?"

He spoke the truth. "I'm no one."

"You expect me to believe that?"

He shrugged carelessly, though every nerve was strung taut. "I don't really care what you believe."

Dakota radiated palpable animosity. She pressed the shirt to Shay's head so hard her knuckles whitened. "Oh, that's right. You're the too-cool cowboy who doesn't care about anyone or anything. You're just in it for the payout."

Shay groaned. "I feel like my head's gonna explode. Can you both please shut up?"

"Sorry." Dakota eased up on the pressure. She glared at Logan, her expression seething. "We're not done here."

He stared back at her, eyes steady and hard. He couldn't let her see his guilt. He didn't owe her a thing, certainly not an explanation.

Still, every word she'd spoken struck him straight to the core.

His past was his own. His demons were his own. The darkness that haunted his nightmares must remain in his nightmares. He had to keep it locked down deep. It was the only way he knew how to survive.

He pretended he didn't give a damn what she thought, that the disgust in her gaze didn't fill him with shame and loathing.

Julio raced back into the store, carrying two plastic bags of supplies.

"The gang already cleared out all the good drugs. All they had left was Aspirin," he said apologetically. "I did grab a bottle of Jack Daniel's, though."

Relief thrummed through his whole body. He could already taste the liquor sliding down the back of his throat. It took great effort to resist grabbing the bottle and knocking it back right then and there.

"It's still gonna hurt like hell," Dakota warned Shay.

Shay's features went rigid. Her eyes glittered with pain—and brave determination. "Just get it done."

42
DAKOTA

After she'd downed a good bit of the whiskey, Shay gave Dakota clear instructions.

They sterilized their hands, the scissors, razor, and needle and dental floss with rubbing alcohol.

Dakota removed the plastic bags from her hands. They'd just get in her way during such precise, intricate work. She needed full dexterity—and focus—for this.

"Ready?" Dakota asked.

Shay gave a slight dip of her chin.

Ready enough.

"Irrigate the wound, first," Shay said. "With the water. Got to get out any contaminates...to prevent infection."

"What about disinfecting it?" Julio asked. "Peroxide or iodine? Rubbing alcohol?"

"Booze?" Logan offered.

"Too harsh. Will just...slow down healing process. Water is good."

Still kneeling over her, Dakota poured water over Shay's head while Logan and Julio held her down. Shay let out several low moans of pain.

Dakota's heart pounded against her ribs. She worked quickly but carefully as she cut a large hunk of Shay's blood-matted coils close to her scalp. She carefully shaved as much as she could, until she could see the ragged edges of the wound clearly.

Shay bit down on a pair of new socks Logan had ripped from their packaging. Julio overcame his fear of blood enough to sit beside her and hold her hand.

While Dakota worked, Logan simultaneously daubed the fresh blood from the wound and held the ragged flaps of flesh close together so Dakota could suture them more easily.

"Keep an eye on the exits," Logan told Julio. "Tell me the second you see or hear anything."

Julio nodded. He chanted one of his Catholic prayers over and over, his eyes wide in the flickering shadows.

Shay moaned into the sock several times. She managed to remain remarkably calm considering the pain Dakota was about to inflict on her.

"Take deep, slow, steady breaths," Dakota instructed. "Go somewhere inside yourself, somewhere deep that the pain can't reach. The fear and anticipation are worse than the pain itself. Enduring is just as much mental as physical, okay?"

Sister Rosemarie had taught her that at the compound, when she'd helped Eden care for Dakota after the visits to the mercy room.

One, two, three. Breathe.

It seemed like nonsense, but when it was only you and the agonizing pain that wouldn't stop, pain throbbing through every cell in your body—you did what you had to do.

You endured.

When she glanced up, Logan was watching her intently, a line between his thick dark brows. She didn't have time to wonder what he was thinking—or care.

She'd deal with him later.

Dakota took her own slow, steady breaths as she pierced the needle down through the sub-dermal layer of skin to the left of the wound—deep enough to keep from tearing the skin but not any deeper than necessary—and made an initial holding knot.

Shay flinched and hissed in pain, but she did her best to remain still.

"One, two, three. Breathe."

Shay breathed. She squeezed Julio's hand so hard the tendons stood out on her forearm. A vein pulsed in her throat.

Dakota leveled the needle and carefully wove the thread tightly between the gaping flesh to the adjacent flaps of the wound in a diagonal pattern, then angled the needle to the skin's surface and repeated the zigzag.

Her hands were steady. She'd learned to focus, to push out all distractions to get the job done.

She didn't know a lot about medical stuff, but after Eden had nearly bled out, Ezra had insisted on teaching Dakota how to stitch up a wound herself.

She needed to know how to take care of herself, he used to say constantly. You couldn't always depend on access to ambulances and hospitals.

The world didn't owe anyone anything—not a good life, not healthcare, not even safety.

Whatever you wanted, you needed to be ready and willing to take care of it on your own.

He'd gotten the opportunity to teach her when she'd slipped on peat on a black-bellied whistler duck hunt and landed hard on a submerged log.

A thick, broken branch sliced a three-inch gash on the side of her calf just above her rubber field boots.

He'd made her sew herself up for practice. Of course, she'd had an actual suture kit Ezra had ordered off some survivalist website, with nylon thread and a curved needle.

A sewing needle and dental floss served as a poor substitute. The straight, slim needle was a pain in the ass to work with, but she had no way to curve the needle herself without pliers and intense heat.

But the stitches only needed to hold for a day or so until they got Shay to a functioning hospital.

Dakota pierced Shay's skin with the needle and pulled the floss through carefully, sucking in her breath as her fingers nearly slipped in the slick blood.

Logan did his best to dab the blood away even as he applied pressure with the crumpled shirt in his other hand.

Tension tightened in her chest with every passing second. It was difficult, painstaking work, made even harder by the leaking blood and wavering flashlight. She needed to be quick without doing more damage.

No one spoke as she worked. The only sounds were Shay's shallow breathing and her own heartbeat thumping against her ribs.

She repeated the suture, timing her breaths with each jab of the needle, until the laceration was finally closed. She finished with a closing knot and snipped the floss with the craft scissors Julio had brought.

Dakota sat back and examined her handiwork. The bleeding had nearly stopped. The stitches were a bit ragged, but tight. Not bad. Not bad at all.

She gave a satisfied grin. "It's ugly as hell, but at least your brains won't fall out."

43
DAKOTA

Dakota covered the wound with a sterile gauze dressing while Logan wrapped a bandage of medical tape around Shay's head to keep it in place.

Their fingers touched a few times, and she resisted the urge to jerk her hands back. She was too angry to even look at him.

Shay tentatively touched her half-shaved scalp above the bandage. Her mouth contorted, dismayed tears springing to her eyes.

"Breathe," Dakota said. "One, two—"

"Three." Shay took several deep, steadying breaths. "My hair will grow back. I know that. I'm sure it looks fine."

"You sure about that?" Logan smirked. "You want a mirror?"

She managed a weak smile, but it was genuine. "You know what? I think I'll pass."

Dakota found herself grudgingly impressed. For a beautiful, put-together girl who looked like she'd never suffered anything worse than a bad hair day, Shay was handling this crisis remarkably well.

She was stronger than Dakota expected. Dakota couldn't help but respect the girl's toughness—and like her for it.

Shay grabbed Dakota's hand. "Thank you so much. I know that wasn't easy."

Dakota's first instinct was to pull away, but she forced herself to remain still. She hadn't been touched in kindness—other than by Eden during supervised visits—for over two years.

She wasn't used to it.

Shay's hand trembled slightly, her palm clammy but warm. Her fingers squeezed Dakota's, still slick with blood, then let go.

Dakota gave an uncomfortable shrug. "It was nothing. Really. Let's get you up."

She helped Shay to her feet. The girl swayed a bit unsteadily but stood on her own. She was a few inches taller than Dakota, her wild halo of coils making her appear even taller.

Gingerly, she touched the makeshift bandage wrapped around her head. "Can you watch me for signs of traumatic brain injury and shock? Symptoms like fainting, speech problems, enlarged pupils, cold and clammy skin, and vomiting."

"Of course." Guilt wormed through her. Shay would be fine if she'd stayed back at the theater. Dakota was the reason they were out here in the first place.

But she couldn't focus on that now. Shay was on her feet, wounded but stable.

It was time to go.

Eden was still out there, a little more than two-and-a-half miles northwest. The radiation was one percent of what it was two days ago, but it was still a deadly threat looming over them, an invisible poison invading their flesh.

Dakota glanced at her watch. 1:49 p.m. So much could happen in so little time. It only took a few seconds to change everything.

Like the bomb, forever dividing their lives into *before* and *after*.

"We've already lost well over an hour," she said. "We've got to move."

"Should we split up?" Julio asked. "You and Logan go after your sister, while I get Shay out of the hot zone to look for a hospital?"

"That's a bad idea," Dakota said. "We only have one working gun between us. What if you run into another thug? Or a whole group of them?"

As much as she wanted to travel faster without them, the thought of leaving Julio and Shay alone without protection went against her instincts.

Dakota couldn't leave Shay behind now; the girl needed her help.

She'd brought them out here; at the least, she could ensure they got to an emergency shelter or medical center.

Logan remained silent, his expression indifferent. He probably didn't care what happened to any of them. Or maybe he was simply too drunk to pay attention.

"I'd rather not split up," Shay said. "I feel okay right now."

"As soon as we get my sister, we'll get out of the hot zone and find you a working hospital, okay?" Dakota promised, and meant it.

Shay nodded and flashed her a grateful smile.

"What should we do with him?" Julio pointed back at the unconscious gangbanger.

"He's not going anywhere," Shay said. "The bullet likely broke his scapula and punctured his brachial nerve. He's bleeding out."

Julio's pallor lost even more color. He touched his gold cross. "We're murderers, then."

"Logan's the murderer, not you." Dakota wiped her bloody hands on a clean shirt and disinfected them with a wash of rubbing alcohol. "And a piss-poor one at that."

Julio wrung his hands, looking down at the body with a mix of guilt, pity, and relief. "But the police...we can't just leave a dying man. We should do something, contact someone..."

"Who?" Logan said. "Any cops nearby will be busy with rescue efforts or quelling gang uprisings like this one."

"Don't you get it yet?" Dakota said too harshly. She couldn't help it. They needed to understand. "Everything's changed. The regular rules don't apply anymore."

"She's right." Logan raked his hands through his unruly dark hair. His eyes were black in the beam of the flashlight. "We're on our own."

44
DAKOTA

Dakota studied Julio as he shook his head, still fingering his cross. He didn't get it fully yet, even now. It was hard for normal people to make the adjustment from a world of rules to one where anything goes.

Maybe she was wrong. Maybe as soon as they exited the hot zone, they'd be greeted by volunteers bearing hot soup and hugs, escorted by armed police officers ready to restore order.

Maybe everyone would come together in a time of crisis, putting aside their own selfish needs for the good of the victims, the shattered cities, the nation.

She wasn't going to hold her breath.

Logan retrieved the bottle of Jack Daniels and poured what remained into his silver flask. He took a long swallow, capped it, and shoved it back into his pocket.

She gritted her teeth and resisted the urge to slap it right out of his hands. She still burned with anger at what he'd done.

What use was a hired gun if he was a drunk?

"Isn't it morally wrong to just walk away?" Julio argued. "To just let him die?"

"He would've wasted you without a second thought," Logan said in a gruff voice. "And done worse to Shay."

"He spent the last forty-eight hours exposed to massive levels of radiation," Shay said gently, resting her hand on Julio's shoulder. "I know how you feel. But look at him. His hair's already starting to fall out. He was experiencing vomiting, dizziness, and disorientation. The aggression could've been from cognitive impairment."

Logan grunted. "Or maybe he was just an asshole."

Julio didn't look convinced. He crossed himself, muttering something under his breath, but finally he nodded in surrender.

Dakota squatted in front of the gangbanger and dug in the pocket of his saggy shorts. She pulled out Julio's gold band and handed it to him.

Julio slipped it on his thick finger and pressed his palm to his chest. He closed his eyes and breathed an unsteady sigh of relief. "Thanks. Yoselyn—my wife—she'd never have forgiven me."

"Of course, she would've." Shay clenched her jaw against the pain. "It's you she wants. Safe and alive."

"You don't know her temper," Julio said, but he managed a tight grin.

Dakota reached for the fallen M4 and slung it over her neck and shoulder, positioning the single-point sling so the weapon hung freely but within easy grabbing distance.

Logan stared at her, brows lowered. "You know how to use that thing?"

"Well enough." In truth, she'd shot one a few times but not enough to get truly comfortable. It wasn't like her trusty XD9, which fit her hands like a glove.

But there was no way in hell she was letting Logan have both weapons.

She checked the magazine: empty.

Her stomach sank. Of course, it was.

"Not that it matters," she said with a sigh.

Pushing down her disappointment, she checked Blood Outlaw for extra ammo or additional weapons. He was clean. Nothing useful on him at all. Not a single damn thing.

Hopefully, just the sight of the wicked-looking carbine would scare any potential troublemakers away.

Still, a few bullets would've been damn helpful.

Shay looked askance at the carbine but uttered no complaints. Getting shot tended to change one's priorities pretty quickly.

In this world, weapons were a necessity.

"We still need what we came here for," Dakota said. "Clothes, food, medical supplies. We need to move quickly. We've already wasted too much time."

"All the new clothes are in the back," Julio said.

Through the employee doorway at the rear of the store, they found what they needed: stacks of unopened boxes full of the newest fall designs.

Julio helped Shay hobble inside and leaned her against a wall of shelves. In the windowless room, the only light shone from the single flashlight Julio still held.

"Guess it's a good thing chain stores still deliver cold-weather gear to Florida," Shay mumbled.

Dakota unsheathed her knife, slit each box down the middle, and pulled on an oversized navy-and-white striped shirt with sleeves long enough to fold over her hands.

"This is stealing," Julio said hesitantly. "It feels wrong."

"If it makes you feel better, when all this is over, we'll come back and pay for what we take," she said.

Dakota was no thief—not anymore, not since that first time—but she instinctively understood that everything was different now.

Julio and Shay needed to change their mindset from one of comfort, safety, and morality to the reality of a cold, brutal world without laws or rules.

They were used to a soft life, a life where they could call 911 for instant help. They still expected the police and the government to protect them, expected everything they needed to line the shelves of stores.

Most of all, they expected the old rules of civility to apply.

At least in south Florida, the old world was over. Probably for a long time.

She didn't feel an ounce of guilt for taking what she needed from an abandoned store. The name of the game was survival now.

She found a case of scarves—thin, pretty, meant for accessorizing. They were better than nothing.

"Contrary to popular belief, fallout isn't a significant inhalation hazard because the particles are so large and they fall to the ground quickly," she explained. "The exposure from radiation on the ground is more hazardous than the threat of breathing it in."

She grabbed a pale gray one and wrapped it around her head and the lower part of her face. When she spoke, her voice was slightly muffled. "That being said, I feel better wearing something."

Julio handed Shay a pink and brown plaid scarf. She held it up. "Every little bit helps, right?"

Julio went with forest green checkered with yellow. "We're gonna die from the heat," he muttered.

"Better than dying from the radiation." Logan pulled on a black faux leather jacket and a matching black, fringed scarf.

Shay leaned against the wall, upright but breathing heavily. She managed a weak smile. "At least we'll die stylish."

After she helped Shay exchange her flip-flops for socks and

flat-heeled ankle boots, Dakota doled out the duct tape, carefully taping their ankles and wrists to keep out as many stray particles of radiation as possible.

"What about this for bringing stuff with us?" Julio bent over a freshly opened box and held up an aqua sequined shoulder bag.

It wasn't a quality bug out rucksack, but they could carry some supplies until they found something better.

They stocked up on Air Heads, Pop Rocks, Mentos, and those plastic containers of mini M&Ms, then went to Walgreens and packed more fresh gauze, topical antibiotics, and bandages.

Julio helped Shay as she walked haltingly through Walgreens. Dakota tossed her a bottle of Advil, and she downed eight pills with a few swigs of bottled water.

Shay found a shelf of disinfectant alcohol wipes. She, Dakota, and Logan wiped the dried blood from their hands and faces. Dakota tossed a couple packages of the alcohol wipes into her bag so they could clean off the radioactive dust if they got some on their skin.

The Blood Outlaws or other looters had already cleaned out the medications in the pharmacy, but there was still plenty of Advil and Tylenol, candy, granola bars, and several bottles of water left.

Calories were calories. No one wanted to dally in the hot zone scavenging for food.

Julio stuffed a Three Musketeers in his back pocket and patted his paunch. "Not a good time for dieting, I guess."

No one laughed.

Dakota wasn't the only one who felt the tension thrumming through her veins, the apprehension tightening her chest. The dying thug had left them all shaken, whether they wanted to admit it or not.

They paused for a moment, looking out the broken windows at a world none of them recognized anymore.

Shay straightened her shoulders, her head held high. "Now, we're ready."

Dakota didn't think they'd ever be ready for what lay ahead.

But they didn't have a choice.

The End

AUTHOR'S NOTE

I hope you enjoyed *Point of Impact*! While I tried to be accurate with the setting of Miami, some names and places were adjusted for the sake of the story.

As I researched improvised nuclear devices and their potential for destruction, I found some competing information.

The reality is, we don't know exactly what a nuclear groundburst detonation in a modern urban city would look like.

Hopefully, we never have to find out.

That being said, I tried to be accurate with the nuclear information I included while also being true to the story and the characters.

Thank you so much for reading.

ALSO BY KYLA STONE

Point of Impact

Fear the Fallout

Beneath the Skin

Before You Break

Real Solutions for Adult Acne

Rising Storm

Falling Stars

Burning Skies

Breaking World

Raging Light

No Safe Haven

Labyrinth of Shadows

ACKNOWLEDGMENTS

Thank you as always to my awesome beta readers. Your thoughtful critiques and enthusiasm are invaluable.

Thank you Becca and Brendan Cross, Lauren Nikkel, Michelle Browne, Jessica Burland, Sally Shupe, Janice Love, Jordyn McGinnity, Jeremy Steinkraus, and Barry and Derise Marden.

To Michelle Browne for her skills as a great developmental and line editor. Thank you to Eliza Enriquez for her excellent proofreading skills. You both make my words shine.

And a special thank you to Jenny Avery for volunteering her time to give the manuscript that one last read-through and catch any stray errors. Any remaining errors are mine.

To my husband, who takes care of the house, the kids, and the cooking when I'm under the gun with a writing deadline.

And to my kids, who show me the true meaning of love every day and continually inspire me. I love you.

ABOUT THE AUTHOR

I spend my days writing apocalyptic and dystopian fiction novels. I love writing stories exploring how ordinary people cope with extraordinary circumstances, especially situations where the normal comforts, conveniences, and rules are stripped away.

My favorite stories to read and write deal with characters struggling with inner demons who learn to face and overcome their fears, launching their transformation into the strong, brave warrior they were meant to become.

Some of my favorite books include *The Road*, *The Passage*, *Hunger Games*, and *Ready Player One*. My favorite movies are *The Lord of the Rings* and *Gladiator*.

Give me a good story in any form and I'm happy.

Oh, and add in a cool fall evening in front of a crackling fire, nestled on the couch with a fuzzy blanket, a book in one hand and a hot mocha latte in the other (or dark chocolate!): that's my heaven.

I mean, I won't say no to hiking to mountain waterfalls, traveling to far-flung locations, or jumping out of a plane (parachute included) either.

I love to hear from my readers! Find my books and chat with me via any of the channels below:

www.Facebook.com/KylaStoneAuthor
www.Amazon.com/author/KylaStone
Email me at KylaStone@yahoo.com

Made in the USA
Monee, IL
08 January 2023